SWEET
NOTHING

ALSO BY RICHARD LANGE

Dead Boys

This Wicked World

Angel Baby

SWEET NOTHING

STORIES

RICHARD LANGE

MULHOLLAND BOOKS

Little, Brown and Company

New York Boston London

Copyright © 2015 by Richard Lange

All rights reserved. In accordance with the U.S. Copyright Act of 1976, the scanning, uploading, and electronic sharing of any part of this book without the permission of the publisher constitute unlawful piracy and theft of the author's intellectual property. If you would like to use material from the book (other than for review purposes), prior written permission must be obtained by contacting the publisher at permissions@hbgusa.com. Thank you for your support of the author's rights.

Mulholland Books / Little, Brown and Company
Hachette Book Group
1290 Avenue of the Americas, New York, NY 10104
mulhollandbooks.com

First Edition: February 2015

Mulholland Books is an imprint of Little, Brown and Company, a division of Hachette Book Group, Inc. The Mulholland Books name and logo are trademarks of Hachette Book Group, Inc.

The publisher is not responsible for websites (or their content) that are not owned by the publisher.

Excerpt from "You Came Last Season" by Gregory Corso (page v) copyright © 1955 by Gregory Corso. Reprinted with permission by City Lights Books. Grateful acknowledgment is made to the publishers of earlier versions of these stories: *The Atlantic* Fiction for Kindle, "Must Come Down"; *Slake, The Best American Mystery Stories 2011*, "Baby Killer"; *The Summerset Review*, "The Wolf of Bordeaux"; *The Sun*, "The 100-to-1 Club"; *The Southern Review*, "Gather Darkness"; *New World Writing*, "Instinctive Drowning Response"; *Bull*, "Apocrypha"; *Kenyon Review Online*, "After All"; *Southern California Review*, "Sweet Nothing"; *Alaska Quarterly Review*, "To Ashes."

The Hachette Speakers Bureau provides a wide range of authors for speaking events. To find out more, go to hachettespeakersbureau.com or call (866) 376-6591.

Library of Congress Cataloging-in-Publication Data
  Lange, Richard
  [Short stories. Selections]
  Sweet nothing : stories / Richard Lange.—First edition.
     pages cm
  ISBN 978-0-316-32754-1 (hardback)
  I. Lange, Richard, Must come down. II. Title.
  PS3612.A565A6 2015
  813'.6—dc23   2014019902

10 9 8 7 6 5 4 3 2 1

RRD-C

Printed in the United States of America

For Kim Turner:
"You never washed away
You stained something awful"

"Now, gods, stand up for bastards."

William Shakespeare, *King Lear*

CONTENTS

Must Come Down 3

Baby Killer 29

The Wolf of Bordeaux 58

The 100-to-1 Club 75

Gather Darkness 105

Instinctive Drowning Response 128

Apocrypha 141

After All 168

Sweet Nothing 184

To Ashes 213

SWEET
NOTHING

MUST COME DOWN

I'M PUSHING THE CART out of the supermarket, rolling through the automatic doors, when I decide I want a cigarette. *Need* a cigarette. I've been a good boy for six months, ever since Claire's EPT came up positive. If she couldn't drink or smoke, I wouldn't either. The deal seemed like one a husband should make when his wife is carrying their baby, but suddenly, here in the Vons parking lot, I'm all, *Forget that, got to get me one of those coffin nails.*

The problem is, no one smokes in L.A. I'm there five minutes waiting for somebody to come out of the store and light up so I can bum one, and I finally end up paying a homeless guy fifty cents for a generic. He strikes a match with his filthy hands, and we talk about spy satellites as I lean on my cart, puffing away. He tells me they have this technology now that allows them to look inside your mailbox and peek into your windows from way out in space, and I'm wondering, *Should I care about this?* Because I don't.

The cigarette gives me a headache, and the weather

makes it worse. The kind of hot we're having sucks the sweat out of you even if you're only going to the mailbox. Walk down the hill to 7-Eleven, and you're risking dehydration and death.

Also, Claire's parents are coming. David and Marjorie. For the weekend. That's why Claire sent me here in the first place, to buy all sorts of expensive stuff that we never spring for when it's just us. Lox, shrimp, organic blueberries, fancy coffee. I didn't put up a fight. I could see how nervous she was when I helped her spread clean sheets on the foldout couch this morning. And she's so big these days, so unsteady on her feet with all that added girth. She always looks like she's about to cry, like she's shocked at how gravity has turned against her.

Because of this I find myself agreeing to things we'd definitely have gone toe to toe over before she got pregnant, even though a buddy of mine warned me against such retrenchments. He said that once you give up ground, getting it back is a bitch. But I'm not sure I trust his advice. He and his wife divorced three months after their baby was born, and everything is war to him now.

I smoke the cigarette to the filter, drop it to the pavement, and twist it out. Then, reaching into one of the grocery bags, I grab whatever comes to hand first.

"You like pâté?" I ask the homeless guy.

He grimaces. "Pâté?"

"It's good," I say, "here," and give him the can.

"Don't you have any beer?" he says.

★   ★   ★

"DON'T YOU HAVE any beer?"

This is from David, Claire's dad, a couple of hours later. He and Marjorie have just arrived, and I've walked them out of the sweltering apartment and onto our little deck overlooking Echo Park. Claire has brought champagne for the two of them and sparkling cider for us. Truthfully, I'm with Dad. I'd kill for a beer right now, and another cigarette, but I laugh with Claire when Marjorie whispers, "David!" and I lift my glass of cider and smile when David makes a toast to family.

We sit at the table on the deck and dig into the imported crackers and twenty-dollar cheese that Claire has arranged ever so carefully on a silver serving platter that we argued about for three days when I happened upon the receipt. The conversation goes pretty smoothly, considering that this is only the second time I've met David and Marjorie, the first being at our wedding, a year ago. I don't know much about them except that they're rich and constantly on the move. Paris, New York, Singapore. Right now they're en route to Hong Kong.

"So how are you feeling?" Marjorie asks Claire, reaching over to brush aside a lock of hair that has fallen across her daughter's forehead.

"Fat. Ugly. Stupid," Claire replies.

"What a thing to say," David snaps. "Don't you know how blessed you are?" He turns to me. "What a thing for her to say."

I shrug and try to make a joke. "Well, she sure is hungry. A whole pint of Ben and Jerry's in one sitting. This kid's going to come out looking like a sumo wrestler."

David ignores me, turns back to Claire.

"You're not fat, and you're not ugly," he says. "You're blessed."

Back when Claire and I were first going out, I asked her what her dad did, and she said, "Something with diamonds, some kind of broker." How he put it at the rehearsal dinner was "I'm a middleman, a person who knows lots of people. If you have a gem you want to sell, you come to me. If you want to buy a gem, I can also help you there. Nothing too exciting."

This seemed sketchy to me, but then so do half the jobs our friends have: consultant, aggregator, brander. Not that I have any room to talk. I still tell people I work in production when all I ever did was PA on a couple of commercials right after I got out of film school. What I really am is a part-time substitute teacher. And Claire, for the record, is not in wardrobe; she owns a little thrift store on Sunset that would have gone out of business ages ago if David didn't send a check every month.

"What are you going to do when the baby comes?" David says.

"What do you mean?" Claire replies.

He gestures toward the apartment. "There's only one bedroom. You need a nursery."

"The baby will sleep in our room. It'll be fine."

David turns to me and raises a wise finger. "Buy yourself some earplugs," he says. "You don't even know."

My dad cut out before I was walking, moved to Dallas, halfway across the country. I saw him maybe five or six times growing up—a day here, a weekend there—and not at all in the past ten years. And my stepfather, he was the quiet type, let my mom do the raising. What I'm saying is, if this is an example of fatherly wisdom—buy earplugs—I guess I didn't miss out on much. I don't even like his tone. How does he know what I know? And talking about the size of a person's home right in front of him—there must be a rule against that somewhere.

LUCIFER, CLAIRE'S CAT, won't leave me alone. I'm on my iPad in the living room, playing this game I'm hooked on, where you maneuver a soap bubble through a narrow cavern studded with stalactites and stalagmites, and the goddamned kitty keeps butting me with his big black head and purring so loudly that he seems to be doing it just to be annoying.

The bubble pops again, and I give up and lie down on the couch. Lucifer sits on my chest and does that strange kneading thing with his paws. Claire and her mom are at Ikea, and David is napping in the bedroom. I can hear his snores over the noise of the fan I've got trained on me.

Okay, so this place *is* kind of a dump. The plaster walls are cracked, the floor feels spongy beneath your feet, and when the guy in the next unit takes a leak, he sounds like he's using our toilet. But we've got the hills. We've got the trees and the lake and the park. I tried to explain this to David earlier, and he laughed and said, "And the gangs and the graffiti and the midnight gunshots." That made me wonder what Claire had been telling him behind my back. I mean, having a baby was her idea, and so was the idea to have it *here*.

But I don't want to be that kind of person anymore—blamers, Claire calls them—so I push the cat off and go into the kitchen. Maybe some dishes need washing. Sometimes giving myself over to ritual is helpful.

I'm up to my elbows in soapy water when David strolls in wearing boxers and a wife-beater and carrying a joint.

"Do you get stoned?" he says.

I back away from the sink, confused. I could answer his question in a couple of ways, and I want to choose the right one.

"Not in a while," I say as I grope for a towel to dry my hands.

"I've got a prescription. Migraines," he says. "But I hate to smoke alone. Come have a puff."

"I don't know about that," I say, but at the same time I'm excited, like I'm in high school again, cutting shop with the cool kids to weed up under the bleachers.

"Who are you worried about?" David says. "Claire? Marjorie? Get with it, guy."

You didn't convince me. That's what I want to tell David as I follow him out onto the deck. *I decided on my own.* That's what I want him to understand, but no nice way to say it comes to mind.

He lights the joint with a green plastic disposable and

takes a long drag. He's about sixty, a little taller than me, a lot heavier. Not fat. Beefy. He still has muscle. He passes me the joint, then reaches up to smooth his fringe of white hair, lips pursed as he holds in the smoke. His already ruddy face flushes even redder.

I go easy, take in a lot of air, but still double over coughing.

David exhales with a loud whoosh and shakes his head. "You're kidding, right?" he says.

My wife's father egging me on. And just the other day I told myself that everything strange that was ever going to happen to me probably already had. David makes me hit the joint again before he'll take it back. I feel the high in my feet first, then it begins to move up my legs.

"The Respighi tonight should be something," David says.

We're going to the Hollywood Bowl, a box down in front courtesy of one of Marjorie's old sorority sisters from UCLA. I've only been once before, with a group of friends from a bar I used to haunt. We sat in the cheap seats and drank too much wine. The ushers kept shushing us, and Mikey B puked in the bushes on our way down the hill. I woke up embarrassed the next morning and swore again that I was going to change my life.

Respighi. *Pines of Rome.* With fireworks. "I'm looking forward to it," I say to David, as if I know something about classical music.

Without consulting each other, we sit at the same time at the little table on the deck. The heat isn't bad here, tucked away in the shade as we are, but my body is running slightly behind my brain. I know this because I think about taking my pulse for a good five seconds before my right hand actually moves over to discreetly grasp my left wrist.

I needn't be so stealthy. David has forgotten all about me. He's staring down at the park, at the paddleboats on the lake, humming a four-note tune over and over. My fingers locate a throb, but I have no idea how many beats per minute are normal.

"This is good stuff," David says.

I nod, then wonder if he saw me. "Great," I say, to make sure.

A noisy black bug flies in out of nowhere and circles us twice. David pops up out of his chair to swat at it.

"What's that?" he says, his voice rising toward panic. "A bumblebee? A cockroach?"

The bug veers off into the bushes. David smooths his hair again and says, "Let's go for a walk. I'm claustrophobic."

I glance at my watch. Two p.m. I last checked at 1:55, what seems like an hour ago. A walk. Sure. We need to get things moving again.

THE LAKE IN Echo Park isn't a real lake, but on the right days it's as pretty as one. Today isn't one of those days, however. Today the water lies there, black and viscous, not a sparkle, not a ripple, and McDonald's cups and Doritos bags founder in the shallows, where a few greasy ducks make gagging sounds as they struggle to stay afloat. The tall palms scattered around the park sport more dead fronds than live ones, and the downtown skyscrapers in the distance have been eaten up by the smog.

David and I sit on a bench and suck Mexican popsicles. Watermelon, with seeds and everything. The vendor who sold them to us was a short, round man with a cowboy hat and gold bridgework. A puff of cold air escaped from his pushcart when he opened the lid, and I wanted to crawl inside and never come out.

The initial jolt of the weed has passed, and now I'm just plain stoned, so the popsicle tastes great, but I'm still paranoid that everyone knows we're wasted. I sit up straight and make sure I don't stare at anything too long. David obviously doesn't have the same worries. He slouches on the bench and keeps removing his sunglasses to reveal his bloodshot blue eyes.

The park is crowded with people in search of a respite from the heat. Women push strollers, drunks snooze open-mouthed on the grass, and teenage couples in black hoodies and spiked belts work joylessly at giving each other hickeys. The song blaring from the nearest radio is a ballad in Spanish about a man who misses a river.

"It's like Tijuana down here," David says. "Like Mexico City."

"You'll probably see more Guatemalans," I say. "Salvadorans, Nicaraguans, Filipinos."

David waves away this comment. "You know what I mean," he says.

I do, but I enjoy busting his balls.

"Talking about Guatemala, I was there once," he continues. "I drove an RV from Phoenix to Costa Rica back in the seventies, passed through all those Central American hellholes. The police pulled me over in Guatemala for driving without a shirt on."

"Without a shirt?" I say.

"Apparently it's against the law there, or at least it was that day. One of the bastards wrote *$20* on a scrap of newspaper and handed it to me, and I went nuts. 'Fuck you!' I said. 'I'm not giving you anything.' I started the RV, put the pedal to the metal, and left them standing there with their dicks in their hands. Last I saw, they were laughing so hard they could barely stand up."

I don't say *Liar, liar,* but I'm thinking it. Or maybe the dude is actually crazy, pulling a stunt like that. I start laughing because I can't think of anything else to do. David laughs too.

"I had hair down to my ass back then," he says between guffaws.

What the hell, let the man spin a few yarns. That check of his hits the mailbox like clockwork the first of every month, and Claire and I would be sunk without it. I only worked five days in June, barely enough to pay the interest on our Visa.

I bite down on my popsicle, tear off a big chunk. A toddler breaks free from his mom and makes a bowlegged dash for the lake. *Stand up,* I tell myself, *do something,* but David is already there. He grabs the kid's arm just as he's about to tumble into the water and then swings him up into the air.

"Careful, Panchito," he says.

The boy's mother is more upset than she should be. She's gasping for air, practically weeping, when David hands the kid back to her. "Thank you, thank you, thank you," she says.

"De nada," David replies, patting the kid on the head and returning to the bench.

He's looking at me and wondering what kind of father I'm going to be if I couldn't even rouse myself to stop that kid. I don't blame him. I worry all the time that parenting is an instinct some people have and some don't, and because my dad didn't, I might not either. Claire tells me I'm being ridiculous, assures me that I'll do fine, but that's only because she's so unsure of herself. Look around you: parents fail every day, and half the people you meet were ruined by the time they were twelve.

"Koreatown is near here, isn't it?" David says.

"Not too far," I say, happy to move on to something else.

"I'm supposed to have a drink with a friend. He'd probably get a kick out of meeting my son-in-law."

"You mean now?" I say. "I'm kind of—" I put my fingers to my lips and mime a joint.

"You're okay," he says. "A drink will straighten you out."

A church bell rings somewhere, and I lift my foot to warn away a strutting pigeon that's getting too close. This is the first time David has referred to me as his son-in-law, and I feel I owe him something. It's a feeling I'm not sure I like, but nonetheless I say, "Yeah, cool, let's go."

★   ★   ★

I WAS NERVOUS about meeting David and Marjorie that first time, at our wedding. They were Jewish; I wasn't. They had money; I didn't. Claire had gone to Yale; I hadn't. "Relax," Claire said. "They're not like that." She and I had been dating for a year, and she'd visited her parents only once, flying over to spend a week in Switzerland with them. I hadn't seen my own mother in ages, but I'd always thought rich families were different.

Marjorie was great, a little ditzy but sweet. As long as Claire was happy, she was happy, and will someone please bring me one of those crab things being served right now, and another glass of wine while you're at it?

David, however, was a different matter. I sensed disapproval, but he didn't actually say anything disapproving; I don't know if he'd been told to keep it to himself or if he'd decided on his own that he shouldn't comment on his daughter screwing up her life when he'd pretty much checked out of it years earlier, when she'd left home for college.

Our one extended conversation was about Clint Eastwood. David had met him at a golf tournament and been very impressed. "You should make a film with *him*," he said. When I went to shake his hand after Claire and I exchanged vows in a friend's backyard, he put his arms around me, hugged me tightly, and said, "Give love to get love."

"Is that a song?" I asked Claire later.

"A sucky one, if so," Claire said.

I went over it in my head for weeks, wondering if that was the best he could do or if he wasn't even trying.

THE BAR IS called the Alps. It's shoehorned into a crowded mini-mall at Sixth and Berendo, between a dry cleaner and a tofu restaurant. David parks his rental in the lot and checks himself in the rearview mirror. He's wearing a black polo and pressed khakis. I asked if I should dress up, and he said a shirt with a collar would be fine.

We're the only non-Asians in the place, which is decorated to evoke a mountain cabin, with skis and poles and snowshoes hanging on the knotty-pine paneling next to large photos of snow-covered peaks. A fire is burning in the circular fireplace in the middle of the room, surrounded by couches. The air conditioner is turned all the way up to compensate for the heat of the flames.

The place has lots of customers for so early in the afternoon, mostly well-dressed middle-aged men drinking in groups of three or four. They watch warily out of the corners of their eyes as David leads the way to the bar and motions for me to sit. The bartender is a beautiful Korean girl in a tight red dress. She ignores us, polishing wineglasses until David calls her over.

"What'll you have?" he says to me.

"I'm not really drinking these days," I reply.

"Get something so you don't stand out," he whispers, then turns back to the bartender. "Two Johnnie Walker Blacks on the rocks."

While the drinks are being poured, he nods to a little man with a complicated comb-over who is sitting by himself in a booth. The man nods back ever so slightly, then pulls out a phone and makes a call. Signals are definitely being sent and received in here. I can hear them whizzing through the air around me. Some kind of work is getting done.

The bartender sets the scotches in front of us, and I take a big sip and try to look hard. David downs half of his in a gulp and says, "I should remember, I know, but how did you and Claire meet again?"

It's a filler question, one he presumes I'll have a long answer to that'll eat up the next few minutes. He wasn't even looking at me when he asked it; he was watching the man in the booth. Him thinking I'm such a chump that I can't see right through him should make me angry, but it doesn't. I get the idea that he's counting on me to play my part in whatever he's got cooking, and I don't want to let him down.

Of course, the story I give him about Claire and I being introduced by a mutual acquaintance and gradually growing closer during a series of dinner and movie dates is complete crap. In reality, we met at a downtown bar, and I fucked her standing up in an alley two hours after I bought her a drink.

A couple of buddies who'd done her and dumped her in the past warned me that she'd get too serious too quickly, but I was coming off a string of psychodramas starring women who'd left me feeling like I'd been beaten and robbed, and a bit of stability sounded appealing.

Turned out Claire was as sick of her life as I was of mine, and that's where we connected in the beginning. We teamed up to build our own thing, us against the world, carving out a new space and tossing aside any junk from our pasts that didn't fit. We lost friends, we burned bridges, but we told ourselves it was the price of progress.

And now, here we are. Mission accomplished. Married, baby on the way, cool apartment in a cool neighborhood, eating right, no more binges, no more soul suckers, no more morning-afters, yet I still wake terrified some nights and spend long, lonely hours in the dark conjuring up demons and disasters and torturing myself with the knowledge that everything we have could be snatched away from us as quickly as the wind blows out a candle.

David says, "That's how it usually goes, I guess," when I finish giving him the sanitized version of how Claire and I came together. Then he continues: "Marjorie and I fought like wild animals for the first few years. We almost killed each other before we learned to get along. I'm glad you two had an easier time of it."

He finishes his scotch, bouncing the ice off his teeth. I'm halfway through mine, and it's gone to my head. This is dangerous because I'm a mean drunk. A few belts, and I get a mouth on me. The mirror behind the bar is covered with that spray-on snow you use on Christmas trees, and someone has scrawled something in Korean on it. I have to stop myself from calling the bartender over and asking her what it says.

"How do you like teaching?" David asks, another ques-

17

tion he's not interested in the answer to. Before I have a chance to respond, the man in the booth stands and walks over to us.

"Hello, Mr. Song," David says.

"Hello, Mr. Friedman," Mr. Song says in heavily accented English. "So nice to see you."

"This is my son-in-law, Haskell," David says.

"Pleased to meet you," Mr. Song says to me.

"Pleased to meet *you*," I reply, feeling like we're reciting a dialogue from a language class.

"Can I buy you a drink?" David says.

"No, thank you. I must attend to some business," Mr. Song says. "However, I do have the information you requested."

He passes David a slip of paper with an address written on it.

"Thank you very much," David says. "Are you sure I can't get you something?"

"I'm sure," Mr. Song says. "I must be going."

We finish up with handshakes and bows, and Mr. Song takes his leave, waving to the bartender and shouting something in Korean on his way out.

"What was that?" I say to David after another sip of scotch.

"What was what?" he replies.

I tell myself to slow down, think things through, but, as I mentioned, I get mouthy. "I'm not an idiot," I say.

The only sign that David is irritated is a quick tightening of his jaw. It's enough to back me off.

"Mr. Song is the friend I was telling you about," David says. "I'm sorry he couldn't stay longer."

"Me too," I say.

David reaches over and flicks my glass with his finger, a strangely menacing gesture. "We should get going," he says.

I nod and down my drink, finally accepting that I'm just along for the ride. And you know what, something in that is immensely freeing.

How do I like teaching? I hate it. I hate the kids, who hate me back; I hate the other teachers, both the bitter burnouts and the deluded idealists; and I hate the principals. I hate the classrooms for their fluorescent sterility, and yet I'm filled with scorn when I enter whatever room I'm assigned to and see the regular instructor's attempts to personalize the space: the inspirational posters, the photos of smiling students, the drooping houseplants. I hate the desks, I hate the pencils, I hate the blackboards.

Why do I continue to do it, then? Because I'm too lazy to look for something else I might end up hating even more. And I stay part-time rather than going on full- so I'll be free to take any film gigs that come my way, even though five years have passed since I've been on a set. I used to tell myself I was going to put together something of my own, a short that would serve as a calling card, but I get sleepy as soon as I pick up a pen or open Final Draft.

At least I'm not alone. Lots of folks are spinning their wheels. Being nothing special is nothing special.

★   ★   ★

THE CAR IS hot enough to boil blood. David starts the engine and turns on the air conditioner. Two men are smoking cigarettes in a patch of shade in front of the bar, and I think about asking for one. The traffic report comes on the radio. Everything is a mess in every direction. David lights the joint we were working on earlier and takes a hit. He doesn't offer it to me.

"One more stop," he says as he puts the car in reverse. "It's not far."

We drive to another mini-mall, this one on Olympic, and park in front of a shoe store. At least, I think it's a shoe store. All the signs are in Korean.

"Do me a favor," David says. "Go in there and pick out some shoes and send the owner back to pull your size."

"What for?"

"I want to surprise him. He's another old friend."

This is a lie, but I'm afraid of how David will react if I ask again what we're really up to. I'm going to have to trust that he wouldn't drop his son-in-law, his daughter's husband, the father of his grandchild, into anything too shady.

"Pick out some shoes," I say.

"That's it," David says.

A chime sounds when I walk into the store, but the owner, staring at a laptop behind the counter, doesn't look up. He continues to ignore me as I wander around the store. There's nothing here I'd actually buy. All the styles are a little off—too shiny, too pointy. I eventually settle on a crazy pair of tasseled loafers made of green suede.

The owner glares at me when I set the shoes on the counter.

"How about these in a ten?" I say.

The guy mumbles something under his breath, then slinks through a doorway into a back room stacked to the ceiling with shoe boxes. The chime sounds again, and I look over my shoulder to see David coming into the store with a finger to his lips. He motions to the front door and mouths, *Wait in the car,* then hurries over to stand with his back to the wall beside the entrance to the storeroom.

Before I can move, the owner reappears carrying a box. David reaches out and throws a choke hold on the guy, who drops the shoes and struggles to free himself.

"Get in the fucking car!" David yells as he drags the owner back into the storeroom.

I've chosen sides or been chosen or whatever, and I can't switch now. The heat comes down on me like a hammer when I step out of the store, and my legs are shaking. Anybody looking at me would suspect that I was up to no good, but luckily the parking lot is deserted. I move quickly to the car, open the door, and fall into the passenger seat.

The scotch has turned into a snake in my gut, one that's trying to slither its way back up my throat. I take out my phone and scroll madly through the names and numbers. *Hello, Claire? Your dad is beating the shit out of some guy in a shoe store in Koreatown. Should you have maybe told me something before you left me alone with him? Hello, 911? Get me out of here.*

The worst part is, I saw the whole business coming and could have sidestepped it but didn't. So nothing's changed. Wife, baby, Diet Coke instead of whiskey, and still I stand there grinning like an idiot as trouble bears down on me and wonder if it'll feel any different when it hits this time.

The owner walks out the front door with David right behind him. The owner's hair is mussed, and a twist of bloody toilet paper protrudes from his left nostril. David glances at me while the guy is locking up the store, and I sneak my phone back into my pocket. The two of them approach the car. David opens my door and says, "Mr. Lee is going to navigate."

I climb out and move into the back. Mr. Lee sits stiffly in the passenger seat, staring out the windshield. Waves of rage and humiliation ripple off him. David starts the car and drives out of the parking lot. One of his knuckles is oozing blood. He checks on me in the rearview, his icy blue eyes searching for weakness. I do my best not to give anything away.

"Where to?" he says to Mr. Lee.

IN THE YEARS between my father leaving and my mother marrying my stepdad, Mom dated a number of men and even let a few move in. I liked those who played Star Wars with me and let me watch R-rated DVDs and showed me how to load and shoot a .22. Others weren't so great: the one who made me go to Sunday school with the neighbors so he and my mom could have "alone time"; the one who punched me in the stomach when I scratched his truck with my bicycle.

And then there was Bill. He was one who stayed with us for a while, his excuse being that he was waiting for a big check the government owed him. He was a cocky, long-legged redhead just out of the navy who had lots of great stories about serving on the USS *Nimitz*. He'd call me sailor, and I'd snap to attention and shout out, "Aye, aye, Captain."

One day he and I went to Walmart while my mom was at work. Two security guards stopped us on our way out and patted Bill down. Unbeknownst to me, he'd swiped a screwdriver, two Snickers bars, and a pack of D batteries. The guards searched me too, and I couldn't stop crying, because I was sure I was going to jail. Bill hung his head when they laid into him. What kind of man shoplifts with a kid, they wanted to know. "A dumbass," Bill said. "A real dumbass." One of the guards prayed with him, then they snapped his picture and let us go without calling the police.

Bill begged me not to tell my mom what had happened, said it was some pills he was on that made him forget to pay. I'd never had an adult ask for my loyalty before, so I gave it wholeheartedly. A week later he snuck off while Mom and I were at the grocery store, taking our TV with him.

Aye, aye, Captain, you son of a bitch.

WE TAKE A short drive to a duplex on Normandie, a run-down heap with faded wood siding and bars on the windows. A pack of kids are kicking a soccer ball in the dirt yard and shouting at one another in Spanish when we pull up in front. David and Mr. Lee open their doors and get out of the car. I stay where I am, hoping they'll forget about me. When David leans in and says, "I need your help, Haskell," I say, "I'm not doing anything illegal."

David frowns and thumbs a bead of sweat from the tip of his nose. "Nothing illegal is going on here," he says.

If I refuse, things might turn even uglier. That's my thinking as I leave the car and follow David and Mr. Lee to the side of the building and up a rickety staircase that leads to the entrance to the second-floor unit. At least if I'm there, I can get between them.

Mr. Lee unlocks the door to the apartment, and we walk into the kitchen. The cabinets are all wide open, and flies buzz around a dirty rice cooker sitting on the counter. The place smells like garlic and rose-scented air freshener.

"Wait here," David says to me. He and Mr. Lee go down the hall, turn into another room, and close the door.

I flip through a calendar that's stuck to the refrigerator. Each month has a different photo of Korea: a neon-drenched cityscape, a stone temple, a group of women in colorful robes. I imagine Mr. Lee, homesick while he waits for his rice to get done, sitting with his head in his hands at the little kitchen table and wishing he hadn't given up on Seoul. A picture of Jesus hangs on the fridge too, and a Pollo Loco coupon.

The sounds of a scuffle drown out the shouts of the kids playing in the yard. Someone is slammed against a wall once, twice, three times, and the apartment shakes like it's about to come down on us. The door in the hallway opens, and David steps out. He storms back into the kitchen, red-faced and breathing hard.

"Go in there and tell him this is his last chance," he whispers. "Say that you're afraid of what'll happen if he doesn't give me the money."

"What money?" I say.

"He owes me for a stone."

"David—" I begin.

"Look," he says. "This is it. If you can't get him to pay, the matter moves up the chain, and next week the poor bastard will have a squad of ex-Mossad on his ass."

I close my eyes and shake my head. David could be lying, or he could be telling the truth. Right now, I don't care; I just want to get out of here. I leave the kitchen without another word and walk down the hall.

Mr. Lee is sitting on the edge of an unmade bed, smoking a cigarette. The room is a mess. The dresser has been tossed; so has the closet. Clothes are everywhere, papers, pillows.

I gesture at Mr. Lee's cigarette and say, "Can I have one?"

He nods toward a pack of Kools lying on the floor. I pick it up, pull one out, light it with the book of matches tucked into the pack's cellophane. I deliver David's message pretty much as he told me to, and I'm not fibbing when I say that I don't know what he'll do if he doesn't get what he wants.

Mr. Lee stares down at the worn carpet between his feet.

He's trying his damnedest not to cry. A tear gets away from him and slides down his cheek. He finally points without looking to a heater vent on the wall.

WE'VE DROPPED MR. LEE back at the shoe store, and David is a happy man. He switches the radio from news to classic rock and bobs his head in time to the music. A big grin spreads across his face. He lifts the collar of his shirt to his nose, hoots loudly, and says, "Wow, I stink."

I stare out the window, watching the buses and the wheelchair bums and the blowing trash with new appreciation. The Earth is flat, and I wandered too close to the edge. I'm glad to be back on the map.

"I'm sorry you had to see how the sausage gets made," David says.

"Does Marjorie know you beat people?" I ask. "Does Claire?"

David's smile disappears. "I don't beat people," he says. "That wasn't a beating."

At a red light he reaches into his pocket and pulls out a wad of money. He peels off three hundred–dollar bills and holds them out to me.

"Keep it," I say.

"What, you like it better when it comes in a check every month?" he says.

He thinks he's got me there. A real Big Daddy moment, a real life lesson. But hypocrisy is the least of my worries. I have plenty of other good stuff to hate myself for.

See, you can't teach anybody anything, David. That's the one conclusion I've come to as a substitute. All you can do is present the information, and the student has to make the choice to learn. And what you're laying down, I already know. Yes, we're all con men at heart, and, yes, the world is a swamp of misery and avarice. But what I'm searching for, David, what I need, is someone to show me how to live in it.

THAT NIGHT AT the Bowl, Marjorie hands me her phone and tells me to take a photo of her, David, and Claire with the orchestra onstage behind them. She and David each place a hand on Claire's belly for the picture. Our seats are right in front, close enough to see the musicians' brows furrow when they play difficult passages, close enough to watch them flex their fingers during pauses. But still, the pounding of my heart drowns out the music.

Everybody in the boxes around us is drinking champagne, everybody's having fun. I hand the phone back and turn to gaze at the upper tiers where I sat last time. I remember looking down here and wondering, *Who the hell are those people?*

I excuse myself and walk to the refreshment stand, where I use one of David's hundreds to buy two shots of Jack Daniel's. I down them quickly, then move to another window and order two more. The fist inside my chest unclenches a bit, and I notice stars overhead, lots of them, shining hard in the dingy purple sky.

Claire smells the booze on me when I get back. Worry clouds her pretty face. "What's going on?" she whispers.

She's gotten used to me tiptoeing these last few months. She's forgotten what kind of person I really am. I put my arm around her and squeeze her shoulders.

David, watching from the other side of the box, interprets this as a romantic gesture. He nods approvingly and raises his Korbel in tribute to young love. Anger dries my mouth and stiffens my spine. I want to twist him as much as he twisted me today. I lean forward so that only he can hear me, and, gesturing at Claire and myself, I say, "This is where I fuck this up."

His eyes narrow to slits.

"What?" he barks.

I reload and get ready to repeat myself, but just then the fireworks go off, making us all jump. The orchestra surges, every instrument roaring at once, and the music finally explodes inside me and whips the tatters of my sick, sick soul. Yes! What a riot.

BABY KILLER

PUPPET SHOOTING THAT BABY comes into my head again, like a match flaring in the dark, this time while I'm wiping down the steam tables after the breakfast rush at the hospital.

Julio steps up behind me with a vat of scrambled eggs, and I flinch like he's some kind of monster.

"*¿Qué pasa?*" he asks as he squeezes by me to drop the vat into its slot.

"Nothing, *guapo*. You startled me is all."

I was coming back from the park yesterday and saw it happen. Someone yelled something stupid from a passing car; Puppet pulled a gun and fired. The bullet missed the car and hit little Antonio instead, two years old, playing on the steps of the apartment building where he lived with his parents. Puppet tossed the gun to one of his homeys, Cheeks, and took off running. He shot that baby, and now he's going to get away with it, you watch.

Dr. Wu slides her tray over and asks for pancakes. She

looks at me funny through her thick glasses. These days everybody can tell what I'm thinking. My heart is pounding, and my hand is cold when I raise it to my forehead.

"How's your family, Blanca?" Dr. Wu asks.

"Fine, Doctor, fine," I say. I straighten up and wipe my face with a towel, give her a big smile. "Angela graduated from Northridge in June and is working at an insurance company, Manuel is still selling cars, and Lorena is staying with me for a while, her and her daughter, Brianna. We're all doing great."

"You're lucky to have your children close by," Dr. Wu says.

"I sure am," I reply.

I walk back into the kitchen. It's so hot in there, you start sweating as soon as the doors swing shut behind you. Josefina is flirting with the cooks again. The girl spends half her shift back here when she should be up front, working the line. She's fresh from Guatemala, barely speaks English, but still she reminds me of myself when I was young, more than my daughters ever did. It's the old-fashioned jokes she tells, the way she blushes when the doctors or security guards talk to her.

"Josefina," I say. "Maple was looking for you. *Andale* if you don't want to get in trouble."

"*Gracias, señora,*" she replies. She grabs a tray of hash browns and pushes through the doors into the cafeteria.

"*Qué buena percha,*" says one of the cooks, watching her go.

"Hey, *payaso,*" I say, "is that how you talk about ladies?"

"*Lo siento, Mamá.*"

Lots of the boys who work here call me Mamá. Many of them are far from home, and I do my best to teach them a little about how it goes in this country, to show them some kindness.

AT TWELVE I clock out and walk to the bus stop with Irma, a Filipina I've known forever. Me and Manuel Senior went to Vegas with her and her husband once, and when Manuel died she stayed with me for a few days, cooking and cleaning up after the visitors. Now her own Ray isn't doing too good. Diabetes.

"What's this heat?" she says, fanning herself with a newspaper.

"And it's supposed to last another week."

"It makes me so lazy."

We share the shade from her umbrella. There's a bench under the bus shelter, but a crazy man dressed in rags is sprawled on it, spitting nonsense.

"They're talking about taking off Ray's leg," Irma says.

"Oh, honey," I say.

"Next month, looks like."

"I'll pray for you."

I like Ray. Lots of men won't dance, but he will. Every year at the hospital Christmas party, he asks me at least once. "Ready to rock 'n' roll?" he says.

My eyes sting from all the crap in the air. A frazzled pigeon lands and pecks at a smear in the gutter. Another swoops down to join it, then three or four smaller birds.

The bus almost hits them when it pulls up. Irma and I get a seat in front. The driver has a fan that blows right on us.

"I heard about the baby that got killed near you," Irma says.

I'm staring up at a commercial for a new type of mop on the bus's TV, thinking about how to reply. I want to tell Irma what I saw, share the fear and sorrow that have been dogging me, but I can't. I've got to keep it to myself.

"Wasn't that awful?" I say.

"And they haven't caught who did it yet?" Irma asks.

I shake my head. No.

I'm not the only one who knows it was Puppet, but everybody's scared to say because Puppet's in Temple Street, and if you piss off Temple Street, your house gets burned down or your car gets stolen or you get jumped walking to the store. When it comes to the gangs, you take care of yours and let others take care of theirs.

There's no forgiveness for that, for us not coming forward, but I hope—I think we all hope—that if God really does watch everything, He'll understand and have mercy on us.

Walking home from my stop, I pass where little Antonio was shot. The news is there filming the candles and flowers and stuffed animals laid out on the steps of the building, and there's a poster of the baby too, with *RIP Our Little Angel* written on it. The pretty girl holding the microphone says something about grief-stricken parents as I go by, but she doesn't look like she's been sad a day in her life.

★　　★　　★

THIS WAS A nice block when we first moved onto it. Half apartments, half houses, families mostly. A plumber lived across the street, a fireman, a couple of teachers. The gangs were here too, but they were just little punks back then, and nobody was afraid of them. One stole Manuel Junior's bike, and the kid's parents made him bring it back and mow our lawn all summer.

But then the good people started buying newer, bigger houses in the suburbs, and the bad people took over. Dopers and gangsters and thieves. We heard gunshots at night, and police helicopters hovered overhead with searchlights. There was graffiti everywhere, even on the tree trunks.

Manuel was thinking about us going somewhere quieter right before he died, and now Manuel Junior is always trying to get me to move out to Lancaster where he and Trina and the kids live. He worries about me being alone. But I'm not going to leave.

This is my little place. Three bedrooms, two bathrooms, a nice, big backyard. It's plain to look at, but all my memories are here. We added the dining room and patio ourselves; we laid the tile; we planted the fruit trees and watched them grow. I stand in the kitchen sometimes and twenty-five years falls away like nothing as I think of my babies' kisses, my husband's touch. No, I'm not going to go. "Just bury me out back when I keel over," I tell Manuel Junior.

Brianna is on the couch watching TV when I come in,

two fans going and all the windows open. This is how she spends her days now that school's out. She's hardly wearing anything. Hoochie-mama shorts and a tank top I can see her titties through. She's fourteen, and everything Grandma says makes her roll her eyes or giggle into her hand. All of a sudden I'm stupid to her.

"You have to get air-conditioning," she whines. "I'm dying."

"It's not that bad," I say. "I'll make some lemonade."

I head into the kitchen.

"Where's your mom?" I ask.

"Shopping," Brianna says without looking away from the TV. Some music-and-dancing show.

"Oh, yeah? How's she shopping with no money?"

"Ask *her*," Brianna snaps.

The two of them have been staying with me ever since Lorena's husband, Charlie, walked out on her a few months ago. Lorena is supposed to be saving money and looking for a job, but all she's doing is partying with old high-school friends — most of them divorced now too — and playing around on her computer, sending notes to men she's never met.

I drop my purse on the kitchen table and get a Coke from the refrigerator. The back door is wide open. This gets my attention because I always keep it locked since we got robbed that time.

"Why's the door like this?" I call into the living room.

There's a short pause, then Brianna says, "Because it's hot in here."

I notice a cigarette smoldering on the back step. And what's that on the grass? A Budweiser can, enough beer still in it to slosh. Somebody's been up to something.

I carry the cigarette and beer can into the living room. Lorena doesn't want me hollering at Brianna anymore, so I keep my cool when I say, "Your boyfriend left something behind."

Brianna makes a face like I'm crazy. "What are you talking about?"

I shake the beer can at her. "Nobody's supposed to be over here unless me or your mom are around."

"Nobody was."

"So this garbage is yours, then? You're smoking? Drinking?"

Brianna doesn't answer.

"He barely got away, right?" I say. "You guys heard me coming, and off he went."

"Leave me alone," Brianna says. She buries her face in a pillow.

"I don't care how old you are, I'm calling a babysitter tomorrow," I say. I can't have her disrespecting my house. Disrespecting me.

"Please!" Brianna yells. "Just shut up."

I yell back, I can't help it. *"Get in your room,"* I say. "And I don't want to see you again until you can talk right to me."

Brianna runs to the bedroom that she and her mom have been sharing. She slams the door. The house is suddenly quiet, even with the TV on, even with the windows open. The cigarette is still burning, so I stub it out in the kitchen sink. The truth is, I'm more afraid for Brianna than mad at her. These young girls fall so deeply in love, they sometimes drown in it.

I CHANGE OUT of my work clothes into a housedress, put on my flip-flops. Out back, I check my squash, my tomatoes, then get the sprinkler going on the grass. Rudolfo, my neighbor, is working in the shop behind his house. The screech of his saw rips into the stillness of the afternoon, and I smile when I think of his rough hands and emerald eyes. There's nothing wrong with that. Manuel has been gone for three years.

I make a tuna sandwich for myself and one for Brianna, plus the lemonade I promised. She's asleep when I take the snack to the bedroom. Probably faking it, but I'm done fighting for today. I go back to the living room and eat in front of the TV, watching one of my cooking shows.

A knock at the front door startles me. I go over and press my eye to the peephole. There on the porch is a fat white man with a bald, sweaty head and a walrus mustache. When I ask who he is, he backs up, looks right at the hole, and says, "Detective Rayburn, LAPD." I should have known, a coat and tie in this heat.

I get nervous. No cop ever brought good news. The detective smiles when I open the door.

"Good afternoon," he says. "I'm sorry to bother you, but I'm here about the boy who was killed yesterday, down at 1238?"

His eyes meet mine, and he tries to read me. I keep my face blank. At least I hope I keep it blank.

"Can you believe that?" I say.

"Breaks your heart."

"It sure does."

The detective tugs his mustache and says, "Well, what I'm doing is going door to door and asking if anybody saw something that might help us catch whoever did it. Were you at home when the shooting occurred?"

"I was here," I say, "but I didn't see anything."

"Nothing?" He knows I'm lying. "All that commotion?"

"I heard the sirens afterward, and that's when I came out. Someone told me what happened, and I went right back inside. I don't need to be around that kind of stuff."

The detective nods thoughtfully, but he's looking past me into the house.

"Maybe someone else, then," he says. "Someone in your family?"

"Nobody saw anything."

"You're sure?"

Like I'm stupid. Like all he has to do is ask twice.

"I'm sure," I say.

He's disgusted with me, and to tell the truth, I'm disgusted with myself. But I can't get involved, especially not with Lorena and Brianna staying here. A motorcycle drives by with those exhaust pipes that rattle your bones. The detective turns to watch it pass, then reaches into his pocket and hands me a card with his name and number on it.

"If you hear something, I'd appreciate it if you give me a call," he says. "You can do it confidentially. You don't even have to leave your name."

"I hope you catch him," I say.

"That's up to your neighborhood here. The only way that baby is going to get justice is if a witness comes forward. Broad daylight, Sunday afternoon. Someone saw something, and they're just as bad as the killer if they don't step up."

Tough talk, but he doesn't live here. No cops do.

He pulls out a handkerchief and mops the sweat off his head as he walks away, turns up the street toward Rudolfo's place.

MY HEART IS racing. I lie on the couch and let the fans blow on me. The ice cream truck drives by, playing its little song, and I close my eyes for a minute. Just for a minute.

A noise. Someone coming in the front door. I sit up, lost, then scared. The TV remote is clutched in my fist like I'm going to throw it. I put it down before Lorena sees me. I must have dozed off.

"What's wrong?" she says.

"Where have you been?" I reply, going from startled to irritated in a second.

"Out," she says.

Best to leave it at that, I can tell from her look. She's my oldest, thirty-five now, and we've been butting heads since she was twelve. If you ask her, I don't know anything about anything. She's raising Brianna different than I raised her. They're more like friends than mother and daughter. They giggle over boys together, wear each other's clothes. I don't think it's right, but we didn't call each other for six months when I made a crack about it once, so now I bite my tongue.

I have to tell her what happened with Brianna, though. I keep my voice calm so she can't accuse me of being hysterical; I stick to the facts: A, B, C, D. The questions she asks, however, and the way she asks them make it clear she's looking for a reason to get mad at me instead of at her daughter:

"What do you mean, the back door was open?"

"She acted guilty? How?"

"Did you actually see a boy?"

It's like talking to a lawyer. I'm all worn out by the time I finish the story and she goes to the bedroom. Maybe starting dinner will make me feel better. We're having spaghetti. I brown some hamburger, some onions and garlic, add a can of tomato sauce, and set it to simmer so it cooks down nice and slow.

Lorena and Brianna come into the kitchen while I'm chopping lettuce for a salad. They look like they've just stopped laughing about something. I feel myself getting angry. What's there to joke about?

"I'm sorry, Grandma," Brianna says.

She wraps her arms around me, and I give her a quick hug back, not even bothering to put down the knife in my hand.

"That's okay, *mija*."

"From now on, if she wants to have friends over, she'll ask first," Lorena says.

"And no beer or smoking," I say.

"She knows," Lorena says.

No, she doesn't. She's fourteen years old. She doesn't know a goddamn thing.

Brianna sniffs the sauce bubbling on the stove and wrinkles her nose. "Are there onions in there?" she asks.

"You can pick them out," I say.

She does this walk sometimes, stiff arms swinging, legs straight, toes pointed. Something she learned in ballet. That's how she leaves the kitchen. A second later I hear the TV come on in the living room, too loud.

"Who was he?" I whisper to Lorena.

"A boy from school. He rode the bus all the way over here to see her."

She says this like it's something cute. I wipe down the counter so I don't have to look at her.

"She's that age," I say. "You've got to keep an eye on her."

"I know," Lorena says. "I was that age once too."

"So was I."

"Yeah, but girls today are smarter than we were."

I move over to the stove, wipe that too. Here we go again.

"Still, you have to set boundaries," I say.

"Like you did with me?"

"That's right."

"And like Grandma did with you?" Lorena says. "'Cause that worked out real good."

We end up here every time. There's no sense even responding.

Lorena got pregnant when she was sixteen and had an abortion. Somehow that makes me a bad mother, but I haven't figured out yet how she means to hurt me when she brings it up. Was I too strict, or not strict enough?

As for myself, the boys went kind of nuts for me when I turned fourteen. I wasn't a tease or anything; they just decided I was the one to get with. That happens sometimes. I was the oldest girl in my family, the first one to put my parents through all that. My dad would sit on the porch and glare at the guys who drove past hoping to catch me outside, and my mom walked me to school every day. I got a little leeway after my *quinceañera,* but not much.

Manuel was five years older than me. I met him at a party at my cousin's when I was fifteen. He'd only been in the U.S. for a few years, and his idea of dressing up was still boots and a cowboy hat. Not my type at all. I was into lowriders, *pendejos* with hot cars. But Manuel was so sweet to me, and polite in a way the East L.A. boys weren't. He bought me flowers, called twice a day. And after my parents met him, forget it. He went to Mass, he could rebuild the engine in any car, and he was already working at the brewery, making real money: they practically handed me over to him right there.

Our plan was that we'd marry when I graduated, but I ended up pregnant at the end of my junior year. Everything got moved up then, and I never went back to school. My parents were upset, but they couldn't say much because the same thing had happened to them. It all worked out fine, though. Manuel was a good husband, our kids were healthy, and we had a nice life together. Sometimes you get lucky.

I DO THE dishes after dinner, then join the girls in the living room. The TV is going, but nobody's paying attention. Lorena is on her laptop, and Brianna is texting on her phone. They don't look up from punching buttons when I sit in my recliner. I watch a woman try to win a million dollars. The audience groans when she gives the wrong answer.

I can't sit still. My brain won't slow down, thinking about Antonio and Puppet, thinking about Lorena and Brianna, so I decide to make my rounds a little early. I can't get to sleep if I haven't rattled the lock on the garage door, latched the gate, and watered my flowers. Manuel called it "walking the perimeter."

"Sarge is walking the perimeter," he'd say.

The heat has broken when I step out into the front yard. The sun is low in the sky, and little birds chase one another from palm tree to palm tree, twittering excitedly. Usually, you can't hear them over the kids playing, but since the shooting, everybody is keeping their children inside.

I drag the hose over to the roses growing next to the chain-link fence that separates the yard from the sidewalk.

They're blooming like mad in this heat. The white ones, the yellow, the red. I lay the hose at the base of the bushes and turn the water on low, so the roots get a good soaking.

Rudolfo is still at work in his shop. His saw whines, and then comes the *bang bang bang* of a hammer. I haven't been over to see him in a while. Maybe I'll take him some spaghetti.

I wash my face and put on a little makeup. Lipstick, eyeliner; nothing fancy. Perfume. I change out of my housedress into jeans and a nice top. My stomach does a flip as I'm dressing. I guess you could say I've got a thing for Rudolfo, but I think he likes me too, the way he smiles. And for my birthday last year he gave me a jewelry box that he made. Back in the kitchen, I dig out some good Tupperware to carry the spaghetti in.

Rudolfo's dog, Oso, a big shaggy mutt, barks as I come down the driveway.

"*Cállate, hombre,*" Rudolfo says.

I walk to the door of the shop and stand there silently, watching Rudolfo sand a rough board smooth. He makes furniture—simple, sturdy tables, chairs, and wardrobes—and sells it to rich people from Pasadena and Beverly Hills. The furniture is nice, but awfully plain. I'd think a rich woman would want something fancier than a table that looks like it belongs in a farmhouse.

"Knock-knock," I finally say.

Rudolfo grins when he looks up and sees me standing there.

"*Hola,* Blanca."

I move into the doorway but still don't step through. Some men are funny. You're intruding if you're not invited.

"Come in, come in," Rudolfo says. He takes off his glasses and cleans them with a red bandanna. He's from El Salvador, and so handsome with that Indian nose and his silver hair combed straight back. "Sorry for sawing so late, but I'm finishing an order. That was the last little piece."

"I just came by to bring you some spaghetti," I say. "I made too much again."

"Oh, hey, *gracias. Pásale.*"

He motions for me to enter and wipes the sawdust off a stool with his bandanna. I sit and look around the shop. It's so organized, the lumber stacked neatly by size, the tools in their special places. This used to crack Manuel up. He called Rudolfo the Librarian. The two of them got along fine but were never really friends. Too busy, I guess, both working all the time.

Rudolfo takes the spaghetti from me and says, "Did that cop stop by your house today?"

"The bald one?" I say.

"He told me he's sure someone saw who killed that baby."

Someone who's just as bad as the killer. I know. I run my finger over a hammer sitting on the workbench. If this is what he wants to talk about, I'm going to leave.

"Are things getting crazier," Rudolfo continues, "or does it just seem that way?"

"I ask myself that all the time," I reply.

"I'm starting to think more like *mi abuelo* every day," he

says. "You know what he'd say about what happened to that baby? 'Bring me the rope, and I'll hang the bastard who did it myself.'"

I stand and brush off my pants.

"Enjoy the spaghetti," I say. "I've got to get back."

"So soon?"

"I wake up at two thirty to be at the hospital by four."

"Let me walk you out."

"No, no, finish what you were doing."

Puppet and his homeys are hanging on the corner when I get out to the street. Puppet is leaning on a car that's blasting music, that *boom boom fuck fuck* crap. He's wearing a white T-shirt, baggy black shorts that hang past his knees, white socks pulled all the way up, and a pair of corduroy house shoes. The same stuff *cholos* have been wearing since I was a kid. His head is shaved, and there's a tattoo on the side of it: *Temple Street*.

I knew his mom before she went to prison; I even babysat him a couple times when he was young. He went bad at ten or eleven, stopped listening to the grandma who was raising him and started running with thugs. The boys around here slip away like that again and again. He stares at me now like, *What do you have to say?* Like he's reminding me to be scared of him.

Baby killer, I should shout back. *You ain't shit.* I should have shut the door in that detective's face too. I've got to be smarter from now on.

★   ★   ★

I HAVEN'T BEEN sleeping well. It's the heat, sure, but I've also been dreaming of little Antonio. He comes tonight as an angel, floating above my bed, up near the ceiling. He makes his own light, a golden glow that shows everything for what it is. But I don't want to see. I swat at him once, twice, knock him to the floor. His light flickers, and the darkness comes rushing back.

My pillow is soaked with sweat when I wake up. It's guilt that gives you dreams like that. Prisoners go crazy from it, rattle the doors of their cells and scream out confessions. Anything, anything to get some peace. I look at the clock, and it's past midnight. The sound of a train whistle drifts over from the tracks downtown. I have to be up in two hours.

I pull on my robe to go into the kitchen for a glass of milk. Lorena is snoring quietly, and I close her door as I pass by. Then there's another sound. Whispers. Coming from the living room. The girls left something unlocked, and now we're being robbed. That's my first thought, and it stops the blood in my veins. But then there's a familiar giggle, and I peek around the corner to see Brianna standing in front of a window, her arms reaching through the bars to touch someone—it's too dark to say who—out in the yard.

I step into the room and snap on the light. Brianna turns, startled, and the shadow outside disappears. I hurry to the front door, open it, but there's no one out there now except a bum pushing a grocery cart filled with cans and newspapers down the middle of the street. Brianna is in tears when I go back inside, and I'm shaking all over, I'm so angry.

"So that talk today was for nothing?" I say.

My yelling wakes Lorena, and she finds me standing over Brianna, who is cowering on the couch.

"Let her up," Lorena says.

She won't listen as I try to explain what happened, how frightened I was when I heard voices in the dark. She just grabs Brianna and drags her back to their room.

I wind up drinking coffee at the kitchen table until it's time to get ready for work. Lorena comes out as I'm about to leave for the bus. She says that the boy from Brianna's school came to see her again, and she was right in the middle of telling him to go away when I came in. She says we're going to forget the whole thing, let it lie.

"I want to show that I trust her," she says.

"Okay," I say.

"Just treat her like normal."

"I will."

"She's a good girl, Mom."

"I know."

They've beaten the fire out of me. If all they want is a cook and a cleaning lady, fine.

MY STOMACH HURTS during the ride to work, and I feel feverish. Resting my forehead against the cool glass of the window, I take deep breaths and tell myself it's nothing, just too much coffee. It's still dark outside, the streets empty, the stores locked tight. Like everyone gave up and ran away and I'm the last to know. I smell smoke when I get off at the hospital. Sirens shriek in the distance.

Irma is fixing her hair in the locker room.

"You don't look so good," she says.

"Maybe it's something I ate," I reply.

She gives me a Pepto-Bismol tablet from her purse, and we tie our aprons and walk to the kitchen. One of the boys has cornered a mouse in there, back by the pantry, and pinned it to the floor with a broom. Everybody moves in close, chattering excitedly.

"Step on it," somebody says.

"Drown it," someone else suggests.

"No! ¡No mate el pobrecito!" Josefina wails, trembling fingers raised to her lips. Don't kill the poor little thing. She's about to burst into tears.

The boy with the broom glances at her, then tells one of the dishwashers to bring a bucket. He and the dishwasher turn the bucket upside down and manage to trap the mouse beneath it. They slide a scrap of cardboard across the opening and flip the bucket. The mouse cowers in the bottom, shitting all over itself. The boys free it on the construction site next door, and we get to work.

I do okay until about eight, until the room starts spinning and I almost pass out in the middle of serving Dr. Alvarez his oatmeal. My stomach cramps, my mouth fills with spit, and I whisper to Irma to take my place on the line before I run to the bathroom and throw up.

Maple, our supervisor, is waiting when I return to the cafeteria. She's a twitchy black lady with a bad temper.

"Go home," she says.

"I'm okay," I reply. "I feel better."

"You hang around, you're just going to infect everybody else. Go home."

It's frustrating. I've only called in sick three times in my twenty-seven years here. Maple won't budge, though. I take off my gloves and apron, get my purse from my locker.

My stomach bucks again at the bus stop, and I vomit into the gutter. A bunch of kids driving by honk their horn and laugh at me. The ride home takes forever. The traffic signals are messed up for blocks, blinking red, and the buildings shimmer in the heat like I'm dreaming them.

I STOP AT the store for bread and milk when I get off the bus. Not the Smart & Final, but the little *tienda* on the corner. The Sanchezes owned it forever, but now it's Koreans. They're okay. The old lady at the register always smiles and says *"Gracias"* when she gives me my change. Her son is out front, painting over fresh graffiti. Temple Street tags the place every night, and he cleans it up every day.

A girl carrying a baby blocks my path. She holds out her hand and asks me in Spanish for money, her voice a raspy whisper. The baby is sick, she says, needs medicine. She's not much older than Brianna and won't look me in the eye.

"Whatever you can spare," she says. "Please."

"Where do you live?" I ask.

She glances nervously over her shoulder. A boy a little older than her pokes his head out from behind a tree, watching us. Maria, from two blocks over, told me the other day how a girl with a baby came to her door, asking for money. The girl said she was going to faint, so Maria let her inside to rest on the couch while she went to the bathroom to get some Huggies her daughter had left behind. When she came back, the girl was gone, and so was Maria's purse.

My chest feels like a bird is loose inside it.

"I don't have anything," I say. "I'm sorry."

"My baby is going to die," the girl says. "Please, a dollar. Two."

I push past her and hurry away. When I reach the corner, I look back and see her and the boy staring at me with hard faces.

The sidewalk on my street has buckled from all the tree roots pushing up underneath it. The slabs tilt at odd angles, and I go over them faster than I should while carrying groceries. If I'm not careful, I'm going to fall and break my neck. I'm going to get exactly what I deserve.

BRIANNA'S EYES OPEN wide when I step through the door. A boy is lying on top of her on the couch. Puppet.

"Get away from her!" I yell. I mean it to be a roar, but it comes out like an old woman's dying gasp.

He stands quickly, pulls up his pants, and grabs his shirt off the floor. Brianna yanks a blanket over her naked body. As he walks out, Puppet sneers at me. He's so close I can feel heat coming off him. I slam the door and twist the dead bolt.

★　　★　　★

IT WAS ONE month after my fifteenth birthday, and all everybody was talking about was a party some kid was throwing
at his house while his parents were in Mexico for a funeral.
Carmen and Cindy said, "You've got to go. We'll sneak out
together." Stupid stuff, teenagers being teenagers. "You tell
your mom you're staying at my house, and I'll tell mine I'm
staying at yours." We were actually shocked that it worked,
to find ourselves out on the streets on a Saturday night.

The crowd at the party was a little older than we were,
a little rougher. Lots of gangbangers and their girlfriends,
kids who didn't go to our school. Carmen and Cindy
were meeting boys there and soon disappeared, leaving me
standing by myself in the kitchen.

One of the *vatos* came up and started talking to me. He
said his name was Smiley and that he was in White Fence,
the gang in that neighborhood. Boys were always claiming
to be down with this clique or that, and most of them were
full of it. Smiley seemed like he was full of it. He was so
tiny and so cute.

Things move fast when you're that age, when you're
drinking rum and you've never drunk rum before, when
you're smoking weed and you've never smoked weed before. Pretty soon we were kissing right there in front of
everybody, me sitting on the counter, Smiley standing between my legs. I was so high I got his tongue mixed
up with mine. Someone laughed, and the sound bounced
around inside my head like a rubber ball.

Following Smiley into the bedroom was my mistake. I should have said no. Lying down on the mattress, letting him peel off my T-shirt, letting him put his hand inside my pants—I take the blame for all that too. But everything else is on him and the others. Forever, like a brand. I was barely fifteen years old, for God's sake. I was drunk. I was stupid.

"Stop," I hissed, but Smiley kept going.

I tried to sit up, and he forced me back down. He put his hand on my throat and squeezed.

"Just fucking relax," he said.

I let myself go limp. I gave in because I thought he'd kill me if I didn't. He seemed that crazy, choking me, pulling my hair. Two of his homeys came in while he was going at it. I hoped for half a second they were there to save me. Instead, when Smiley was finished, they did their thing too, took turns grinding away on a scared little girl, murdering some part of her that she mourns to this day.

Afterward they made me wash my face and get dressed. I wasn't even crying anymore. I was numb, in shock.

"White Fence," Smiley said right before he walked back out into the party, into the music and laughter. "Don't you forget." A warning, pure and simple. An ugly threat.

I never told my friends what happened, never told my family, never told my husband. What could they possibly have said or done that would've helped? Nothing. Not a goddamn thing. The sooner you learn it, the better: some loads you carry on your own.

★　　★　　★

THEY MAKE A big show of it when they come for Puppet. Must be six cop cars, a helicopter, TV cameras. That detective wasn't lying; all it took was an anonymous phone call. "I saw who killed the baby." One minute Puppet is preening on the corner with his homeys, acting like he owns the street, the next he's facedown on the hot asphalt, hands cuffed tight behind his back.

I run outside as soon as I hear the commotion. I want to see. Lorena and Brianna come too, whispering, "Oh my God, what's happening?"

"It's the bastard who shot little Antonio," says an old man carrying a bottle in a bag.

We stand at the fence and watch with the rest of the neighborhood as they lift Puppet off the ground and slam him against a police car. Then, suddenly, Brianna is crying. "No," she moans and opens the gate like she's going to run to him. "No." Lorena grabs her arm and yanks her back into the yard.

"José!" Brianna yells. His real name.

He can't hear her, not with all the shouting and sirens and the *chop chop chop* of the helicopter circling overhead. And I'm glad. He doesn't deserve her tears, her reckless love. Instead, I hope the last thing he sees before they drive him off is my satisfied smile and the hatred in my eyes, and I hope it burns him like fire, night and day, for as long as he fouls this earth.

IT'S FRIDAY EVENING, and what a week. The freezer at work broke down, Maple changed the rules on vacation time, and one of the boys cut his finger to the bone chopping onions. There was some good news too: Looks like Puppet isn't going to be back. As soon as they picked him up, his boy Cheeks flipped on him and told the cops everything. A few punks still hang out on the corner and stare the neighborhood down, but none of them know that it's me who took out their *compadre*.

I fall asleep on the couch when I get home and don't wake up until a few hours later, but that's okay, because I'm off tomorrow, so I can go to bed whenever I want tonight and sleep in. I couldn't do that when Lorena and Brianna were here. They'd be banging around in the kitchen or blasting the TV every time I tried to rest. I'd be cooking for them or doing their laundry.

I love them, but I wasn't sad to see them go when they moved out last week. They're in Alhambra now, living with a fireman Lorena met on the computer. He's really great, she says, with a big house, a swimming pool, and a boat. And so good with Brianna. I was thinking she should ask him about his ex-wife, find out why she's not around anymore, but I kept it to myself.

When I get up, I water the garden and pick a bunch of tomatoes. The sun has just set, leaving the sky a pretty blue, but it's going to be one of those nights when it doesn't cool down until past midnight. The kids used to sleep out in the yard when it was like this. Manuel would cut up a watermelon he'd kept on ice all day, and the juice would run down their faces and drip onto the grass.

I sit on the back porch and watch the stars come out.

There's a little moon up there, a little silver smile in the sky. Oso barks next door, and another dog answers. Music floats over from Rudolfo's shop, old ranchero stuff, and I think, *You know, I'll never eat all those tomatoes by myself.*

Rudolfo looks up from the newspaper he's reading as I come down the driveway, trailed by Oso.

"Blanca," he says. *"Buenas noches."*

He reaches out and turns down the radio a bit. He's drinking a beer, and a cigar smolders in an ashtray on the workbench. He picks up the ashtray, moves to carry it outside.

"Go ahead and smoke," I say.

"You're sure?"

"No problem."

He lived next door for years before I found out he had a wife and son back in El Salvador. He got in trouble with the government there and had to leave. The plan was that he'd go to the U.S. and get settled, then his family would join him. But a few years later, when it was time, his wife decided she was happy where she was and refused to move north. I remember he told this like it had happened to another person, but I could see in his eyes how it hurt him.

"I brought you some tomatoes," I say, setting the bag on the workbench. "I've got them coming out of my ears."

"You want a beer?" he asks.

"Sure," I say and lower myself onto a stool.

He reaches into a cooler and lifts out a Tecate, uses his bandanna to wipe the can dry.

"I'm sorry I don't have any lime," he says as he passes it to me.

"It's good like this," I reply.

He lifts his can and says, *"Salud."*

I take a sip, and, boy, does it go down easy. Oso presses his cold nose against my leg and makes me jump. I'm wearing a new skirt. A new blouse too.

"Another wild Friday night, huh?" I say.

Rudolfo laughs. He runs his fingers through his hair and shakes his head. "I might have a few more in me," he says. "But I'm saving them up for when I really need them."

He asks about Lorena and Brianna, how they're doing at the new place, and wonders if I'm lonely now that they're gone. I admit that I'm not.

"You get used to being by yourself," I say.

"Yeah, but that's not the same as enjoying it," he replies.

I like the way we talk to each other. It feels honest. Things were different with Manuel. One of us always had to win. Husbands and wives do that, worry more about being right than being truthful. What goes on between Rudolfo and me is what I always imagined flirting would be like. It's kind of a game. We hint at what's inside us, each hoping the other picks up on the clues.

I didn't learn to flirt when I was young. I didn't have time. One year after that party I was engaged to Manuel, and the last thing I wanted him to know were my secrets.

A moth flutters against the bare lightbulb suspended above us, its wings tapping urgent messages on the thin glass. Rudolfo tells me about something funny that happened to him at Home Depot, how this guy swiped his shopping cart. It's his story I'm laughing at when he finishes, but I'm also happy to be here with this handsome man, drinking this beer, listening to this music. It feels like there are bubbles in my blood.

A song my mom used to play comes on the radio.

"Hey," I say. "Let's dance."

"I don't know, it's been years," Rudolfo says.

"Come on." I stand and wiggle my hips, reach out for him.

He puts down his beer and wraps his arms around me. I pull him close and whisper the lyrics to the song in his ear as we sway so smoothly together. You forget what that feels like. It seems impossible, but you do.

"Blanca," he says.

"Mmmmmm?" I reply.

"I'm seeing a lady in Pacoima."

"Shhh," I say.

"I've been seeing her for years."

"Shhh."

I lay my head on his chest, listen to his heart. Sawdust and smoke swirl around us. *Qué bonita amor,* goes the song, *qué bonita cielo, qué bonita luna, qué bonita sol.* God wants to see me cry. He must have His reasons. But for now, Lord, please, give me just one more minute. One more minute of this.

THE WOLF OF
BORDEAUX

For Patricia Barbe-Girault

THE NEWSPAPERS CALLED HIM "the Wolf," but his real name was Armand, or perhaps Louis. He gave both when he was captured. He didn't look like a wolf; he looked like a schoolteacher or a customs agent, a clerk of some sort. His hands were soft, his pale eyes unremarkable, and he barely cast a shadow when a light was shined upon him. The authorities said he'd murdered eight children.

"Do you believe them?" he asked me once.

"If they say it's so, it must be so," I replied.

"But of course," he said.

"Shut your mouth," I said.

He dwelled in darkness during his stay in Fort du Hâ, entombed deep in a section of the prison that we called the pit, locked in a dank, miserable cell far from the other inmates. How he wailed when they first brought him in, how he raved, sending up mad, desperate prayers to the saints, then working his way through various devils. He beat his fists bloody on the stones, tore out his hair, and covered himself with his filth.

"A light! A light! Mother! Father! A light!"

I couldn't bear to hear it, had nightmares even, so I offered him a deal: If he'd remain quiet while I was on duty, I'd open the feeding slot in the door of his cell and hang a lantern near it. He readily agreed, and for part of the day, at least, his blackness was broken, and he could see the hell he'd tumbled into.

HE ANGERS ME, I told my commander.

Not for long, my commander replied, drawing a finger across his throat. *Justice will be swift.*

He scares me, I told my wife.

Shhh, my wife replied. *The children can hear you.*

He knows me, I told my priest.

Only God knows you, my priest replied, *while demons seek to deceive.*

WE WERE WARNED not to talk to the men we guarded, especially not those facing the guillotine, "Le Rasoir National." But when you spend hour after hour in that cold, dripping gloom so far from the sun, so far from the pulse of the earth in the grass and the trees, so far from air not freighted with dread and despair, you sometimes need to hear the sound of another voice in order to be reassured that you haven't died yourself and aren't now rotting in your grave.

"*Bonjour,*" the prisoner would say when I opened the slot at the beginning of my watch. "Or perhaps *bonsoir?*"

One morning I finally replied.

"It's day," I said.

"What day?"

"April twentieth."

"Ah, spring is here. And what year?"

"You don't know the year?"

"Time has gotten away from me."

"Still 1899. You've been down here two months."

For the most part we spoke of simple things, he on his side of the door, I on mine. He asked if the hydrangeas had bloomed in the Jardin Public, whether peas were showing up at the market yet, and how high the river was running. This last query disturbed me, because he was said to have thrown the bodies of the children into the Garonne after strangling and mutilating them. I answered without thinking when he asked, however, brooding over the question only later.

"It's running higher than normal," I said.

"What I wouldn't give," he said, "for a plate of lamprey."

As the trial drew near, *La Petite Gironde* printed a list of the victims: Charlotte Le Conte, age ten; Albert Hérisson, age eight; Laure Capdeville, age seven; and so on. Eight in all, though only five corpses had been found. The newspaper reported that the Wolf refused to confirm that the missing children had indeed met death at his hands, thereby denying the grieving parents even the cold comfort of certainty regarding the fates of their sons and daughters. In fact, the bastard hadn't uttered a single word about the crimes, not even to proclaim his innocence.

It made me sick to contemplate. I thought of my own girls, Simone and little Lolo, *mes mignonnes,* and what a horror it would be if they were snatched away from their mother and me. I'm one of those men who are occasionally plagued by bouts of melancholy, and on my worst days back then, my daughters were the only roots I had, my only anchors against a billowing sea of despondence. I imagined the parents of the missing children suddenly lost in houses and on streets they'd known their whole lives. I saw them staring blankly at little beds and little spoons and little shoes and wondering, *How?* and *Where?* and *Why?*

For a few days after the list appeared, the feeding slot in the prisoner's door remained closed. I decided that the beast who'd caused such misery deserved no kindness, no matter how small. I stopped my ears against his pleas for light and passed the long hours of my watch hunting for meaning in the flickering shadows the lanterns threw across the stone walls.

And it was there late one afternoon that I beheld the scales—justice—and a dove—God—and understood that I'd overstepped my bounds, realized that only He has the right to pass judgment. As much as it pained me, I opened the slot again, placed a lantern near it, and fetched a bucket of water so the prisoner could wash himself.

"How long has it been?" he asked.

"Three days," I said.

"Why?"

I passed the list of dead children through the slot. The prisoner glanced at it briefly, then handed it back.

"So I've been found guilty?" he said.

"The trial hasn't started yet," I said.

"Yes, it has," he said.

As I STATED before, for the most part we spoke of the everyday, the mundane, the tiny beautiful details of the world outside, a world the prisoner knew he'd never see again. Occasionally, however, a certain humor came over him and he'd play at reminiscence.

"My father was a butcher, my mother a whore," he told me on one such day. "I was born in the gutter, and the only reason they didn't leave me there is that they needed something to blame.

"My first memory is of my mother sucking off a customer in whatever flophouse we were living in then. My second memory is of my father skinning a rabbit alive and chasing me with its still-kicking, still-screaming carcass, laughing at my pleas that he stop. They kept me in a closet. They used me as a footstool, a garbage pail, a chamber pot. They beat me ceaselessly and with much glee.

"Did your parents beat you?" he asked me.

"Not enough to boast about," I replied.

"I grew to enjoy the brutality," he continued. "At least there was the relief that came afterward, when the blows stopped."

I left the prison that evening thinking I had some insight

into the stresses that twist some men's minds. Imagine my chagrin when, the very next day, the whole story was changed.

"Every Sunday the family sat down to an enormous lunch," the prisoner said then. "Maman, Papa, my brother and sister. The cook labored all morning to prepare the meal, and the serving girl brought in dish after dish after dish. We ate until we couldn't eat anymore, leaving just a bit of room for dessert, of course.

"Then we all went out to the garden, where Papa read his newspapers and Maman dozed over her embroidery while we children played *escargot* and *bilboquet*. At night Maman would tuck me in with three kisses, one on each cheek and the last on my forehead, to sweeten my sleep."

"What's your family name?" I asked, thinking that even though he was lying, he might still slip and reveal some fact that would help the authorities identify him.

"What's yours?" he replied.

"That's not important," I said.

"Exactly," he said.

"And what will it be tomorrow?" I said. "Descended from kings? A gypsy foundling?"

"I've lived many lives," he said. "And I'll live many more."

"I know what you're talking about, and it's blasphemy," I said.

"Really?" he said. "What did you do to get sentenced here?"

"I'm under no sentence," I said. "This is my work."

The prisoner laughed and said, "Nobody would choose this for work. You're being punished for something."

"Something I did in a previous life?"

"Thief," he whispered through the slot in the door of his cell. "Adulterer. Murderer. You dream of your crimes and wake with a stiff prick."

At times like these I had to step away, to retreat down the corridor until I could no longer hear his rants. I didn't want such depravity echoing in my head. I didn't want to take it home with me.

Jean Pissardy, age seven; Irène Dizaute-Lacoste, age eight; Charles Vignes, age eight.

I memorized the list, and the names of the dead and missing came to my lips when they shouldn't have: When I spoke to my daughters, when I kissed my wife, during my prayers. Between that and the vile insinuations the prisoner sometimes spewed, I began to feel that perhaps I *was* being punished for something. Why else would I be more at ease locked in a dungeon with a killer than sharing the boulevards and parks with my fellow citizens?

I turned my face from policemen for fear they'd see in my eyes the disquietude in my soul. I avoided touching the children lest my hands obey some phantom command and do them harm. "Keep your distance," I told my wife and spent my hours away from the prison confined in a cell of my own making, shutting myself up in our darkened bed-chamber, where God and the devil fought over me like two dogs after the same bloody bone.

"WHY DO THEY make you stay down here with me?" the prisoner asked. "Don't they trust their own locks?"

"I'm here to see to it that you don't hurt yourself," I said.

"So that they can hurt me later?" he said.

"Why waste your breath on questions you already know the answers to?" I said.

The prisoner was silent for a second, then said, "Well, have no fear, they're not going to kill this sly one. Right this second Zola is writing a letter for me, just like he did for the Jew Dreyfus. I'll be free in no time."

"No, you won't," I said.

"Yes, I will," he replied.

"If I were you, I'd make peace with what's coming," I said.

When I looked in on him fifteen minutes later, I was shocked to find him hanging from a makeshift noose he'd fashioned from his tunic. He'd somehow wedged the garment into a crevice in the wall so that it would support his weight.

I unlocked the door and entered the cell. Wrapping my arms around the prisoner, I lifted his body until the tunic was no longer taut. He came to sudden kicking, punching life, and I realized he'd merely been feigning unconsciousness in order to draw me inside. I fell back as he wrenched himself free from the wall and stumbled for the door. He was not a big man, nor a strong one, so it was nothing for me to lay my arm across his throat and arrest his flight. I tightened my hold until he ceased his struggles then removed the noose and made him strip off his trousers.

He spent the rest of the day curled naked on his bunk, face to the wall. At the end of my watch I opened the cell door and stood on the threshold.

"If I tell the commander what you did, it'll be a strait-jacket for you," I said.

The prisoner didn't respond.

"I've seen men made crazy by that thing," I continued.

Still no response.

"Can I trust you?" I said.

"Yes," the prisoner mumbled.

"I can't hear you," I said.

"Yes," he pronounced clearly.

I returned his clothes to him and shut the door. He made no more attempts to escape.

A MONTH BEFORE the trial, the prisoner's attorney, accompanied by a clerk and two soldiers, came down into the pit to take his charge's statement. A tall, thin man with a skittish air, the attorney first had me chain the prisoner, then ordered the soldiers to draw their pistols before he entered the cell with a scented handkerchief pressed to his nose. His clerk stood beside him, pad and pen at the ready.

"I am Maître Bergerot, the attorney assigned to the defense in this matter," he said.

The prisoner slouched on his bunk and shot the man a glare that could have driven nails.

"Assigned by whom?" he asked.

"The court," Maître Bergerot answered.

"You look more like an undertaker than an attorney," the prisoner said.

"See here, you bastard——" Maître Bergerot began.

"I see! I see! I see!" the prisoner said, shouting the attorney down.

Maître Bergerot sputtered like flame on damp wood and looked as if he might swallow his tongue. He regained his composure after a few deep draws on his hankie.

"We'll begin again," he said to his clerk, then asked the prisoner his name. The prisoner said he'd heard the newspapers had given him a nickname. Maître Bergerot told him yes, he was being called the Wolf.

"The Wolf will do, then," the prisoner said. "No need to confuse things."

"Listen closely," Maître Bergerot said. "You've been accused of killing eight children. Do you wish to refute these charges?"

"What I'd really like is some lamprey," the prisoner said. "Do you think you could catch one for me, stork?"

Maître Bergerot stared angrily at him, then said to his clerk, "Come. There is nothing I can do for this madman, and nothing I *want* to do but see him pay for his crimes."

"Prepare it *à la bordelaise*," the prisoner called to him as he left the cell. "I'm sure your wife has a nice recipe."

I released him from his chains after the group departed, and he was silent for the rest of the day, a madman, as Maître Bergerot had said, chasing his mad thoughts.

THE SOULS OF children have more worth than the souls of adults, which, sacred though they are, have nonetheless been battered and tarnished by the various degradations encountered along life's rocky path. Thus, if a man who's killed eight men—outside of war, of course, where he'd likely be decorated for such slaughter—if a man who's killed eight men deserves death for his crimes, a man who's killed eight *children* surely deserves death twice over, or thrice, or eight times. Perhaps, in the glorious future we're hurtling toward, some genius will discover a way to return the dead to life again and again, and we'll have true justice at last, as we march our villains to the blade and drop their heads into the basket as many times as is necessary to square their accounts.

I'm not the man for such math, though. I leave that bleak reckoning to the judges and priests, as I lack the certainty required for it. I've known the dark wind that scatters consoling scripture and common wisdom like so many dead leaves, revealing the barren ground beneath. I've wandered lost through a wilderness un-bounded, where no law tempered rage and no morality constrained lust. It was violent and carnal and instantly familiar: my true heart, the true heart of man, and turning from it every time to return home was like tearing myself away from a looking glass.

So, no, I'm not the one to set the sentences. I've seen through the eyes of a snake. I've seen through the eyes of a wolf. I'm too close to beastliness myself to pass judgment. Let me watch over your monsters instead, feeding them, changing the straw in their cells, until the hour comes for them to pay the price that the learned lay upon them.

At the end of the first day of trial, the soldiers assigned to transport the prisoner to and from court returned him to his cell. He was bleeding from a cut on his forehead.

"Did they beat you?" I said.

"No," he said. "It was a stone thrown from the crowd."

Hearing footsteps on the stairs, I quickly moved the lamp away from the door and closed the feeding slot. The commander appeared out of the shadows. I was expecting Pascal, the guard who watched over the prisoner at night.

"Pascal is refusing his watch," the commander said. "The details that came out at the trial have apparently enraged him. I need you to stay on until midnight, when I'll relieve you myself."

"Fine, sir," I said. "If someone would only go around and let my wife know."

"I'll send a man right away, and also arrange for your dinner," the commander said.

"Thank you, sir," I said.

"We'll be rid of this vermin soon enough," the commander said. "Another week or two."

"Yes, sir."

A few hours later I heard someone else descending. This time it *was* Pascal, along with two other guards from another section of the prison. They carried clubs and breathed cheap brandy.

"Step aside," Pascal said. "We mean to take the bastard."

"By whose order?" I said.

"By order of the citizens of Bordeaux," Pascal said. "There are hundreds of them at the gates, demanding satisfaction."

"Satisfaction isn't justice," I said.

"Unlock the door," Pascal said.

"I won't," I said. "And neither will you."

One of the other guards, a sadistic oaf called Dédé, sprang forward and brought his club down on my shoulder with all the strength of his drunken righteousness. The blow shook me to my toes and drove tears into my eyes, but I stood my ground. Dédé raised his club to strike me again and would have cracked my skull if Pascal hadn't stopped him, saying, "Enough, man. He's one of us, after all."

"No, he isn't," Dédé said. "He's a damned coward."

The oaf backed away but looked as if he was waiting for any excuse to continue the beating.

"This scum doesn't deserve your mercy," Pascal said to me.

"I'm a guard, and he's my prisoner," I said. "It's simply my duty to see that he comes to no harm."

Pascal blinked twice and squinted at me, then turned for the stairs. "Let's go," he called to the others. They followed reluctantly, Dédé muttering over his shoulder, "You'll answer to the people for this."

As soon as their footsteps faded, I sank to the ground, my left arm numb, my collarbone throbbing. This was too much for me. If they returned, they could have him, and the devil take them all. It was just me and the rats, though, until the commander arrived and sent me home for the night.

WHERE ARE MY footmen this morning? the prisoner asked.

The trial's over, I replied.

And the verdict? the prisoner asked.

Death, I replied.

What a pity, the prisoner said.

IT TOOK NEARLY a week for the guillotine to be transported down from Paris and erected in the square in front of the fort. The prisoner remained calm until the last day, when a final, furious storm of lunacy left him more lost than ever. I looked in on him at noon and found him pacing his cell. At one he'd stripped off his clothing. At two, he was abusing himself most frantically.

"Tell me about your children," he called out when he sensed me at the feeding slot. "Little girls? Little boys?"

Revulsion like I'd never known nearly doubled me over,

and it was as if I were the first man uttering the first word when I shouted, "Enough!"

"Do you bathe them in the evening?" he continued. "Kiss their little——"

"Another word, and I'll kill you," I said.

"Me? Your dear cell mate?" he said. "I think not." He thrust his free hand through the slot. "Come, brother, let me touch some soft part of you. The underside of your forearm, your eyelids, your tiny cock."

"Enough!" I roared again and laid the hot lantern glass against his grasping fingers. When he pulled them back in pain, I slammed shut the slot and moved off down the corridor, where I begged God to help me douse the fire of my outrage with the blessed waters of compassion.

THE COMMANDER REQUESTED I come in early the next day to assist him in readying the prisoner for execution. The prisoner spent his last hour alone with a priest, and then, at dawn, the commander and I entered the cell. We bound the prisoner's wrists, and the commander cut away the collar of his tunic. Because of the awfulness of his crimes, he was not to be allowed to enjoy the light of his last morning. It was left to me to place the black hood over his head. As I pulled it down, just before it covered his face, I sent him a thought—*I'll pray for you*—but he wouldn't look me in the eye.

★　　★　　★

THAT WAS THE last I saw of him. A trio of soldiers led him to a waiting wagon, which carried him out to the guillotine. I was told he went to his death quietly. The blade fell, the crowd that had gathered to watch cheered, the body was carted away.

The priest returned to the pit shortly after the execution. I sat where I always sat, staring into the empty cell and trying to work up the strength to prepare it for its next occupant.

"You were his guard?" the priest asked me.

"Yes, Father," I replied.

He handed me an envelope. "He asked me to give this to you," he said.

Inside was the list of the Wolf's victims from the newspaper. At the top of the page the prisoner had scrawled the words *Ma Confession,* and next to every name, those of the known dead and those of the missing, he'd written, *Oui.*

I passed the list to the commander. He was pleased, elated even, and told me the rest of the day was mine, a reward for outstanding service. I climbed out of the pit, left the prison, and wandered the early-morning streets in a daze, unused to the bright sunlight and the raucous exuberance of the city coming to life. Women shouted from window to window across narrow alleys, shop owners joked as they set up their sidewalk displays, and children, everywhere children, their joyous voices ringing out like the songs of unseen birds.

I eventually found myself on the steps of Saint-Michel and collapsed there like a weary pilgrim. I'd lived in the shadows of its blackened stones and jagged spires since birth. As a boy I used to imagine that the church was God's armored fist and the tower beside it His sword. One felt safe with something like that always so close. Safe. Oh, how I longed to be a boy again.

Perhaps if I talked to a priest, I thought, he'd have some words of reassurance about the thickness of the walls between worlds and how one can wrestle evil without being infected by it. I wouldn't have believed anything he said, but it might've provided temporary solace, like a soothing balm for a wound that can never heal.

I couldn't bring myself to enter the church just then, however, to return to darkness and heavy silence no matter how sanctified, so I continued to sit on the steps and marvel at the many tiny delights the morning brought my way. The swifts darting so skillfully among the chimneys, the sound of a teacher calling her students to class, the smell of bread from an old woman's basket. And then, both ashamed and unashamed, I bowed my head and wept.

THE 100-TO-1 CLUB

THE SUN HAS NEVER felt as good as it does when I finally step out of that jailhouse and into a beautiful Friday morning, the air smelling a little like jasmine, a little like the ocean; happy weekend smiles on all the faces in the windows of a passing bus; and the mountains sitting right there, like they sometimes do, looking close enough to touch.

I've only been locked up for forty-eight hours, but this bit was worse than any of the others because it was so unexpected. The cops broke into the little casino Kong runs in the back room of his bar, saw the slots and the craps setup, and before you know it, I was being yanked out of my seat at the poker table and slammed against the wall, and when they ran my license, up popped a couple of speeding tickets that had gone to warrant. Two years I'd managed to fly under the radar, and just like that, I was back in the system.

But I'm not going to let it mess me up. I'm going to focus on the things I have to be grateful for—like the fact that Larry's waiting for me out front like he promised he would be, and that he passes me a big old cup of coffee as soon as I slide into his truck, and that he tracked down Domingo and collected the money D owed me and used it to bail me out, all on the back of a single frantic phone call. Unbelievable. You can count friends like that on one hand—hell, one finger.

"Larry, my man," I say. "Let me buy you breakfast."

THE DENNY'S IN the shadow of the freeway next to the jail is the first place a lot of guys go right when they get out, to eat a decent meal and use a toilet with a door. I see a couple of dudes I was in with sitting at the counter—ID bands still on their wrists, property bags at their feet—digging into tall stacks of pancakes and double orders of ham and eggs.

"Tell me what I missed," I say to Larry across the table.

He forks a sausage into his mouth and shrugs. Syrup glistens on his mustache. He's a listener, not a talker.

"Anybody die? Anybody hit it big?" I ask.

"It was only two days," he says.

Yeah, but it sure seemed longer. Probably because I barely slept. The guy in the next bunk moaned and groaned all night, suffering through his dreams, and during the day I was too wound up to nap, surrounded as I was by bad men with bad intentions. I spent all my time guarding my personal space, displaying enough aggression to ward off the jackals but not so much that I riled the tigers. My hands are still shaking. When I lift my glass to drink, orange juice sloshes over the rim.

But back to the good stuff: I'm out, my only friend came through for me, and I've got a date this afternoon with Lupe, a beautiful girl I met last week at this pool hall where I shoot sometimes. We're going to the track, me and her and her kid. She couldn't get a sitter, so I told her to bring him along. "There's all kinds of kids there," I told her. "They love it."

"How's work?" I ask Larry.

He shakes his head. "Picked up a couple days drywalling, but it's slow."

"Let me talk to my cousin. He's looking for help on that house in Eagle Rock."

"You were supposed to talk to him last week."

"Yeah, but then all this went down."

I haven't spoken to my cousin in months because I owe him five hundred dollars. Larry knows this but doesn't call me on it. He's cool like that, always has been. What's crazy is that sometimes I wish he wasn't. Sometimes I wish he'd haul off and punch me in my lying fucking face.

He slurps his coffee and watches the waitress joke with two cops in the next booth. I remember him contemplating joining the LAPD right after he got married, going on and on about the health insurance and the pension plan. He acted like I was some kind of asshole for pointing out that two DUIs and a burglary conviction might hold him back.

"You've got to move out before the first of next month," he mumbles without looking at me. "Shauna put her foot down."

Like I couldn't see this coming. Shauna's been trying to find an excuse to boot me from their garage since the day I moved in.

"We need someone we can count on for regular rent," Larry continues. "We're behind on everything."

The rent bit is bogus. I've only been late once, maybe twice, in almost a year. I haven't paid for April yet, but it's only the fifth, and, guess what, I've been locked down most of that time. Larry could tell Shauna to back off. He could say, *This is my homeboy we're talking about.* But I've been married; I understand. And if me staying there is causing him problems, no sweat. I'll find somewhere else to crash until I get on another roll.

"No worries," I say, and that's enough about that. "So this chick Lupe, the one from Hollywood Billiards—"

"By the first," Larry says, not letting it go.

"Do you think I didn't hear?"

He's given up on me. It's there in his eyes. My hands tighten into fists, and ugly thoughts blaze through my brain. But then I see all the food on my plate and the clear blue sky outside and remember that it's only me who can bring me down, and everything is fine again. Everything's great.

LUPE ALMOST BLEW it for me the night we met. She kept smiling from the bar as I hustled some pigeon, and it was so distracting that, for a while, I thought they were a team. I let the guy take me twice for twenty a game, then came on as drunk and stupid and challenged him to another, this time for a hundred. He figured he had a fish on the line and said, "Whatever you want, bro." I stalled all the way to the eight before putting it away, and then it was him begging for a rematch. I held back in that game too, making my win look like dumb luck. He left grumbling but unable to prove that he'd been had.

His money felt nice in my pocket—easy money always does—and I walked over and introduced myself to Lupe. "Ladies as pretty as you shouldn't be allowed near the tables," I said. "You make it hard to concentrate."

"You still whipped his ass, didn't you?" she said.

"No thanks to you."

She was there with friends from the dentist's office where she worked as a receptionist, somebody's birthday. I bought the group a round with my winnings, but Lupe was the only one I was interested in. The click of the balls faded, the music, everyone else's dopey conversations. All I heard was her voice.

I like Mexican girls. That thick black hair. That brown skin. Those dark, dark eyes, full of secrets. And Lupe had this haughtiness that made me smile because it was such a put-on. She tried to act like nothing meant anything to her, like she was in on the joke, but I could see that was just a shield she was using to protect herself. You win a girl like that over, and you're going to learn what love is all about.

"So what are you," she asked at one point, stabbing her drink with her straw, "some kind of hustler, some kind of shark?"

"Because that's not what you're looking for, right?" I replied. "You're a mom, got a son to think about. You don't need another bad boy messing stuff up."

"Well," she said, "maybe a little bit bad."

When her friends started pulling at her to leave, she took out her phone and asked for my number, then dialed it as I gave it to her.

My phone rang, and I put it to my ear and said, "Hello?" staring right at her.

"This is Lupe," she said. "Call me sometime." And then off she went, swept away by her scandalized *amigas,* one of them whispering, "Oh my God. I can't believe you."

It wasn't going to get any better than that, so I hurried home to Larry's garage, locked the door, and crawled into my sleeping bag before any randomness could ruin a perfect night.

I'M DUE AT Lupe's at noon, which gives me enough time to pick up my Xterra from Kong's, where it's been sitting since I got popped, then drive back to Larry's and sneak a quick shower while Shauna's at the store. The hundred dollars stashed in the toe of one of my good shoes isn't much, but admission is free at Santa Anita today, and they've got dollar sodas and hot dogs, so I should be fine.

Lupe lives in North Hollywood with her sister. The two of them and their kids share a condo. Lupe's sister lived there with her husband, but then he ran off, and when Lupe got rid of her old man, the girls decided to throw in together.

I park in the loading zone in front of the building and give Lupe a call. She'll be down in a minute. While I'm waiting, I walk to the main entrance and look in through the lobby to the swimming pool in the courtyard. The water is perfectly still, and an old man is reading a newspaper at a table with an umbrella sprouting out of it. It's nice, nicer than anyplace I've ever lived.

Lupe and her son walk out of the elevator, and she looks as good as I remember, in tight jeans and a white tank top. The kid is wearing a Spider-Man T-shirt and Spider-Man sunglasses. I try to get the front door of the building for them, jerk it twice before I realize it's locked. Lupe pushes it open from inside.

"They're serious around here, huh?" I say.

"That's right, you lowdown, dirty varmint," the kid growls.

"Jesse!" Lupe snaps, then says to me, "He gets all this weird stuff from cartoons. Half the time I don't even know what he's talking about."

"You like horses?" I ask him.

"Are we gonna ride some?"

"We're gonna watch them race."

"Dag-nab it."

I keep my Xterra immaculate; wash it every week, polish it once a month. It's the only decent habit I picked up from my dad. He couldn't stand it when people paid good money for a vehicle then let it go to pot. "It shows they don't appreciate what they have," he'd say. "That it came to them too easy."

Lupe straps Jesse into the backseat.

"Is there TV in here?" he asks.

"No TV," I say.

"My uncle has TV."

I ignore him. You have to do that to kids sometimes, otherwise they think every silly thing that comes out of their mouths deserves a response. He's all wrapped up in a toy he brought with him anyway, some kind of ninja doll.

Lupe starts right in with a story about a girl she works with who misread the numbers on a lottery ticket and thought she'd won. She got on the phone and screamed to her husband and her mom and danced around the office and promised everyone a cruise.

"I felt so bad for her," Lupe says, laughing and shaking her head. "She called in sick for two days afterward."

I laugh and change lanes to get around a slow-moving semi with its hazards blinking.

"Hey, check it out," Lupe says as we pass the truck.

The semi is hauling four huge palm trees, their roots encased in heavy wooden boxes, fronds tied to their trunks to keep them from blowing around. They look like prisoners on their way to execution. Lupe takes a photo with her phone. She's excited about being out, about the day ahead of us, and maybe even about me. I like that, that she can't hide it.

BY THE TIME we park, it's five minutes to post for the first race. A couple of decent horses are running, and I'd like to get a bet in if I can, but Jesse doesn't know how to hurry yet. He stops to pick up a penny from the pavement, stops again to watch a ladybug crawl. I give up when Lupe kneels to tie his shoe right before we walk through the turnstile, grit my teeth as the announcer calls, "And away they go."

"Would you have won?" Lupe asks when she sees me looking at a tote board a few minutes later.

"Couple a' bucks," I say. "Not enough to cry over."

We pass through the echoey cavern beneath the grandstand, which is full of horseplayers staring up at TV monitors or hunched over copies of the *Form*. The same anxiety that tightened my throat as soon as I drove into the place has these men squinting and licking their lips and slapping rolled-up programs against their palms. This hasn't been fun for any of them for a long time.

Lines have already formed at the betting windows for the next race, and a crowd has gathered beneath one of the TVs to watch a simulcast from San Francisco. "Come on, you motherfucker," a guy in a Raiders jacket shouts at the screen as we walk by. I glance at Lupe and see that she's about to say *Hey, there are kids here* or something, so I rush her outside.

We emerge into the sunlight beside the track, near the finish line. I lead Lupe and Jesse up into the stands and snag three seats. It's ten minutes to post.

"You guys want hot dogs?" I say. "Cokes?"

"Yeah, yeah, yeah!" Jesse chants, bouncing up and down.

Lupe jerks his arm and hisses at him to stop. "One plain and one with ketchup," she says to me.

"Ketchup, ketchup, ketchup," Jesse whispers as I walk away.

*　　*　　*

I HEAD STRAIGHT for a window to put ten on Wilder Thing, the favorite, to win. Then, before I can stop myself, I also put ten on the second favorite. The race goes off while I'm waiting in line at the snack bar, and I watch it on a monitor. My horses come in second and fifth. So I lose, but at least I know how my luck is running. It'll be dollar exactas for the rest of the day, a ten-cent superfecta if the field is big enough.

Paul pops up behind me while I'm ordering the food.

"Get me a dog too," he says, shoving a moist dollar bill into my hand.

"What the fuck?" I say.

"Come on."

Paul is the type of person I need to avoid. He has no goals, no impulse control, no life. Last time I was with him at a card club, we wound up running from some drunk Iranians after one of them accused Paul of trying to lift his wallet. Paul swore up and down they were nuts but then got the crap beat out of him two weeks later for doing the same thing to someone else.

I hand him his hot dog and get no thank-you, nothing, just "You seen Whammy?"

Another lunatic, another crackhead. "Nope," I say. "I got to go."

"What's your hurry?"

"I'm on a date."

"One of them pay-by-the-hour deals?"

The guy hasn't showered in days. His teeth are yellow, and he looks like he dressed out of a dumpster. He follows me to the condiment counter and moves in close as I'm pumping mustard.

"You know somebody looking for something like this?" he says and lifts his T-shirt to flash the butt of a gun sticking out of his jeans. "I'll let it go cheap."

"Who are you?" I say. "I don't even know you."

I push past him, almost spilling the Cokes in my haste. See, I'm learning. That dude is surely going to die young, and I don't want to go down with him.

"Soon as a bitch opens her mouth," a buddy once said, "I stop listening."

Four or five of us were drinking in a dive where failure hung thick as cigarette smoke in the air. Something contrary welled up in me—a sudden, intense disgust at the hatefulness we used for cover—and I pointed out to my friend that I'd seen him talking to women plenty of times.

"Talking, maybe," he said, "but never listening."

I like listening to Lupe. We sit in the stands and eat our hot dogs, and she tells me about her ex, Jesse's father. I asked for details about him because her and I are going to yank out our pasts like weeds and throw them away. The story is a sad one, but she makes it funny by spelling out the words she doesn't want Jesse to hear and calling her ex Dick instead of his real name, so the kid won't know who we're discussing.

They'd been together since high school, and she married him when she got p-r-e-g-n-a-n-t even though she knew he was an a-s-s-hole. Which was stupid, it's clear to her now, because of course the guy cracked under the pressure; of course he couldn't hold up his end of anything. He quit every job he managed to get, f-u-c-k-e-d around on her constantly, and beat on her when he was d-r-u-n-k. She finally had enough of it and got her brothers to come over and throw him out, and every day since then has been a good one.

"I'd like to meet him," I say. "In a dark alley. With a baseball bat."

"He's not worth the trouble," she says.

"He was the wrong man for you," I say. "It's good you found out early."

"Wrong man, right man," she says. "You're all the same."

"No, we're not," I reply. "We come in all kinds of crazy."

This gets a laugh out of her, and we sip our Cokes and watch the horses for the next race parade down the track. A big roan bucks, almost tossing his jockey, and the crowd applauds. I'm transfixed by a man standing half in the shadow of the grandstand and half in the sun, split right down the middle, dark and light. One step in either direction will change everything. *Move,* I think.

"I like number two," Lupe says, wiping ketchup off Jesse's chin with a napkin. "He's pretty."

Toe the Line is the horse's name, three to one.

"You know how to pick 'em," I tell her. "He's one of the favorites."

She reaches into her purse and pulls out two dollars. "I want to bet on him."

I wave the money away. "My treat."

"Nope," she says, thrusting the bills at me. "That's bad luck."

Her smile could stop a war. I take the two bucks and turn to leave. The man I was watching before is gone. If he went light, I'd planned to go with the four horse; dark, the nine. Now I'll have to bet both.

WHEN I GET back from the window with our tickets and a box of popcorn for Jesse, Paul is sitting in the row behind us, leaning forward to talk to Lupe. Something takes hold of my guts and squeezes.

"Here he is," Paul says as I approach. "The man himself."

"Watch your purse around this one," I say to Lupe.

She laughs. Paul looks hurt, then angry.

"She was asking how we met," he says.

Danny Boy brought us together. Gave us the keys to the back door of his brother's house and told us to trash the place, paid us each a hundred bucks. Those were not good times.

"Who can remember?" I say. A warning.

Paul picks up on it. "I can't," he says. "I sure can't."

I give Lupe her ticket, and the kid tries to grab it out of her hand. She tells him to sit still. We make small talk as the horses walk to the starting gate. All I can think of is the pistol in Paul's waistband. It's like there's a snake coiled under

Lupe's seat where she can't see it, and I'm ignoring it so as not to alarm her, all the while terrified that the damn thing is going to strike. Paul's talking about Hawaii, telling Lupe how great it is there: Oh, the sand. Oh, the water. Oh, the food. He's never been to Hawaii; he's never even been to San Diego.

A stiff breeze sweeps up a bunch of losing tickets and whips them around the legs of the Mexicans lining the fence next to the track. The gates swing open, and the horses are off. I'm not normally a stander or a shouter, but Lupe, you know, and the kid, that's part of the fun for them. So as the pack comes into the stretch, I'm on my feet with everybody else, even though my picks are already out of the money.

"I won!" Lupe yells as the horses cross the finish line.

"We won!" Jesse yells.

Lupe hugs him, hugs me, hugs Paul. When things settle down, Paul starts pumping her for info: where she lives, where she works, what she drives. I interrupt with "So, who do you like in the next race?"

"Paul said Kentucky Straight looks good," Lupe replies.

I glance at my program. Thirty-five to one. That's Paul right there: If he can't win, he doesn't want anyone else to. Fucker lives his whole life that way.

"It's a long shot," I say.

"What's that mean?" Lupe asks.

"It means you bet a little to win a lot," Paul says.

"Good, 'cause a little is all I got."

I'm not going to argue. We're supposed to be enjoying

ourselves. And what's two bucks? Paul, though, has got to go.

"Come on," I say to him. "I'll buy you a beer."

"Just bring it to me," he says.

"Nah, come with me. I want to talk to you about something."

He gets up reluctantly, knowing he won't be back, kisses Lupe's hand and bumps fists with Jesse.

As soon as we're out of their sight, I give him a shove. He stumbles and almost goes down. The maniac has a gun, and I push him. I'm a genius; I truly am.

"I don't appreciate your jokes," I say.

"So what?" he says. "She's not that cute. In fact, her ass is gigantic."

I lurch toward him, and he backs off.

"Get going," I say, keeping an eye on his hands.

"You know what?" he says. "I'm done with you." Then he turns and, thank God, walks away.

I DECIDE TO visit Willy and Leon in the clubhouse, see what horses they like. You're supposed to have a stamp to get in from the grandstand, showing you paid extra. I don't, but the woman guarding the entrance is too busy texting to look up when I wave my hand under the black light and hurry past her.

Willy and Leon are legends, twin brothers who worked as pari-mutuel clerks, taking bets here and at Hollywood Park for thirty years before retiring. They still show up every day, out of habit, know all the jockeys, all the owners, all the trainers, and they're usually good for a tip.

I find them in their usual spot, a booth in a quiet corner of the clubhouse snack bar beneath a bank of monitors showing races from all over the country. Five or six other regulars sit with them, and the table is covered with dope sheets, marked-up *Forms*, and Styrofoam coffee cups. The men all wear clothes from twenty, thirty, even forty years ago. They never venture outside to watch a race live, and they communicate with one another mostly in grunts and whispers. Their days are spent scribbling arcane symbols on their programs or staring up at the screens overhead, tongues clenched between their teeth.

At my hello, Willy taps Leon, who takes off his reading glasses and glances around, confused, before spotting me. The brothers are both five feet tall and just about as wide, with big round heads and bulging eyes, and they both comb their graying hair to the same side. The only way anyone can tell them apart is that the lobe of Willy's left ear is missing, sliced off in a gang fight when he was a kid.

"Hey, buddy boy," Willy says. "Keeping out of trouble?"

"You know me," I reply.

"That's why he's asking," Leon says, and he and Willy jiggle with silent laughter. Rumor has it that they've won and lost millions over the years, that they once shared a woman who broke both their hearts, and that they still sleep in their childhood bedroom at their mother's house.

"I need a winner," I say.

"And you came to them?" one of the other men at the

table says with a snort. "They're in so deep, Obama's gonna bail them out."

Everybody gets a kick out of this, one guy laughing so hard he goes into a coughing fit.

"Seriously," Willy says. "It's nothing but nags today."

"Yeah, keep your money," Leon adds.

"Come on," I say. "You guys have something."

They lock eyes for a few seconds, then Willy runs a fat finger down the chicken scratches he's made on a memo pad.

"The five horse in the sixth might come alive," he finally says.

"Might," Leon emphasizes.

Willy announces that he needs to use the can. He's sitting in the center of the booth, which means the guys to one side or the other will have to slide out and stand up, but neither group wants to move. I leave them bickering about it and go to a window, where I cash in Lupe's ticket for eight dollars and put two back on Kentucky Straight.

For my bet, I figure it's been three races now since a favorite has come in, so it's got to happen this time. I mean to lay ten on the horse, but out of habit say twenty and decide not to correct it. I don't want to get in the way of anything.

"COME ON, BABY, come on!" Lupe shouts, but it's no use. Kentucky Straight runs last, and the favorite ends up third. So we're both losers.

"Made for each other," I say to Lupe.

"I'm no loser," she replies.

"It was a joke," I say.

We sit poring over the prospects for the next race when we should be getting to know each other better. This was a horrible place to take her on a first date. I see that now. I'm under too much stress here. Now that I'm down, all I can think about is ways to get back up. And Lupe, look at her, jiggling her leg, twisting her hair, squinting at her program like someone taking a test. The zoo would have been better, something fun for the kid. He's bored to death here, nothing to do but play with his doll, make it jump in the air and kick his mother's arm.

"What's your guy's name?" I ask him.

"Black Dragon."

"So he's like a ninja?"

"Bingo, brainiac."

Shadows are creeping up the foothills just beyond the track, and it'll get chilly as soon as the sun sinks a bit lower. We should leave now, while I still have enough cash to buy us a couple of Big Macs. I'm trying to figure out how to suggest this to Lupe without sounding as lousy as I feel when she jabs her program with a bright pink fingernail and says, "I want this one: Divalicious."

Fifty to one. The girl is throwing away her pennies, but, hey, I don't have any room to talk. She roots around in her purse, hands me two dollars, and says, "What happened with you and your wife?"

It's only fair. She told me about her marriage. But which

story does she want to hear? How Christine and I met at a casino where she was a waitress and I was on a winning streak? That's a good one. Christine thought it was always going to be like that, the high life, and that's why she said yes when I asked her to marry me two weeks later. She'd never been with a gambler before, though, never ridden that roller coaster.

Or how about the one where I had to sell everything we owned to pay off a loan shark, and we lived out of our car until I could pilfer enough from the cash register at the liquor store where I was working to get a room at a motel?

Or how about how I promised again and again to quit gambling but didn't, and when the truth finally dawned on Christine, she texted her good-bye while I was sitting at a poker table — *Thx 4 ruining everything* — and disappeared into outer space?

No, Lupe doesn't want to hear any of those, and I don't want to tell them.

"We made mistakes," I say. "There was love there, but not enough."

Lupe frowns. "What does that mean? Did you leave her, or did she leave you?"

"Me," I say. "She left me. And the man I was then, I don't blame her."

"But you've changed, huh?"

"I get a little better every day, I hope."

"You're full of s-h-i-t," she says with a laugh.

"I know what that spells," Jesse says.

★　　★　　★

THEY'VE BOTH GOT to use the restroom, so I lead them back under the grandstand and thread them through the crowd. We avoid the old woman picking through the trash, the drunk screaming in Spanish into his phone, the dude with crazy eyes who's telling security he'll smoke anywhere he fucking wants. A pigeon has found its way inside and flies frantically from one end of the room to the other, just above everyone's heads.

"Can you go with him?" Lupe says, nodding at Jesse when we get to the door to the women's room.

"Sure," I say.

I take his hand and walk him to the men's. He steps up to the one urinal that's set lower than the others and unzips his pants.

"Need any help?" I ask

"No," he replies, like that's a dumb question.

He can't reach the sink, so I pick him up and hold him around the waist while he soaps his hands and rinses them thoroughly, the way someone somewhere taught him.

"Do you like war?" he asks me while drying each finger separately.

"You mean like *war* war?"

"Like war movies."

"Sure," I say.

"Me too."

We meet his mom at the snack bar, and the two of them wait there while I make our bets. It's going to be the favorite this time: Blue Moon. The guy in front of me puts money on him, and so does the guy in front of him. What I should do is lay down ten of my last twenty on the horse and save ten for Willy and Leon's pick in the next race. But of course the wheels start turning: Lose the ten, and you've got nothing, not enough to make a decent bet on the next race, not enough to buy Lupe and Jesse dinner. Bet the whole twenty, and if you lose, you're still fucked, but if you win, at two to one, that's forty bucks, enough to bet on Willy and Leon's horse and get a pizza, thus tiptoeing out of trouble once again.

By now I'm at the window, and the clerk is waiting, and so is everybody in line behind me. There's no time to double-check my logic, so I do what I always do in this situation: close my eyes and jump.

LUPE SCREAMS LOUDER as the horses come into the stretch. Blue Moon has been in front all the way, but now Divalicious is moving up. I don't want to root against Lupe, not even silently, but I do, fists clenching and unclenching at my sides. Run, run, run.

The crowd is in a frenzy as the horses approach the finish line. It's strange to see people act like that, shouting and sweating and jumping up and down. They look more angry than anything else, and I've had dreams where they turn on me.

The madness continues until Blue Moon and Divalicious cross the line neck and neck at the front of the pack.

Silence descends over the grandstand. It holds for three seconds, four, five, and then the word *Photo* flashes on the tote, and a collective groan rises. Everybody begins to speculate on what the officials will see in the pictures. It looked like Blue Moon to me, but I don't want to jinx it by hoping.

"Oh my God, oh my God," Lupe whispers. She closes her eyes and crosses herself, moves her lips in prayer.

A minute later, the results come up.

"I won?" Lupe asks, her voice rising to a screech.

"You won," I reply.

The old man behind us rolls his eyes as she yells and stamps her feet and waves the ticket over her head. She's got a lot to learn, like how you shouldn't gloat when you win, how you should think about all the losers around you, all those broken hearts.

But, hey, maybe she'll pay for dinner now. I'm down to four bucks and change. I keep reaching into my pockets, hoping to find more, because Leon and Willy's horse, Rocket Man, is starting to look really good. Top jockey, top trainer. He hasn't done anything in his previous races, so that means he's due. And I'm not the only one who thinks so: He's gone from five to one this morning to three to one now. I smell a winner, really and truly.

Jesse drops his Spider-Man sunglasses under his seat, then bumps his chin trying to retrieve them. You'd think he was dying, the way he bawls. The littlest bit of a headache is throbbing at the base of my skull, and it's like the kid is back there kicking it.

"What's wrong?" Lupe asks Jesse.

He cries even harder.

She grabs his arm, yanks him onto his seat, and takes a quick look at his chin. "Stop showing off," she says. "You keep it up, and I'm not buying you a present with this money. I'll spend it all on myself."

The sobs subside into whimpers.

"Should we go?" I ask Lupe, hoping she'll say yes.

"Nah, he's just tired. He'll be fine," she says. She starts to tell me another work story, something about a man crying while getting a molar pulled, but I'm barely listening. I'm too busy beating myself up for not being able to hold back any money for this race, the one where I actually have a decent tip. I can't make the right move even with someone holding my hand.

"Hey," Lupe says, distracted by something on her program. "Did you see? The Tooth Fairy? I have to bet on him."

Seventy to one. One lucky pick, and she thinks she's magic. I could use this as my excuse for what's about to happen, claim she's gotten too full of herself, showed her ugly side, but that would be unfair. She's just a girl who hit a winner and liked how it felt. I'm the one who's rotten through and through.

I STEP UP to the window at two minutes to post. The clerk has a thin gray mustache and a mop of curly gray hair that might be a wig. A big ring shines on his pinkie, and a diamond stud glints in his ear. With his black vest and white shirt, he puts me in mind of a riverboat card shark.

He runs Lupe's ticket through his machine. The payout is $108.80. I have him apply two dollars of that to a win bet on Tooth Fairy.

"How do you want the rest?" he says. "Twenties okay?"

The horses have reached the gate. Mine will be the clerk's last wager for this race. I've waited until now so that whatever decision I come to will be final. You could second-guess the move I'm thinking of making forever, and it's going to haunt me whichever way it goes. It's going to change the things I say to myself when I can't sleep.

"Sir?" the clerk says.

I barely get the words out: "Give me a hundred to win on five."

The clerk repeats the bet as he types it in, then hands me $6.80 in change and closes his window. We're gambling now, friends. I spin the cylinder and press the revolver to my temple. If Rocket Man wins, Lupe will never know I borrowed from her. If he loses—he can't lose. I don't even want to put that out there.

I feel like my skin is two sizes too small, like I'm going to rip if I move too fast. I make my way gingerly to the nearest bar, spend Lupe's change on vodka. The race starts as I raise the glass to my lips.

The announcer's voice bounces wildly in the cavern beneath the grandstand. "Rocket Man," I hear, but that's all I can make out. I move closer to a blurry monitor and crane my neck with the other men standing there. Rocket Man is in front, he's in front, and then he's not. The favorite has finally come in, and Rocket Man is a distant third.

Pow! My brains are all over the table. I finish the vodka and hurry to the exit leading to the parking lot. Lupe, Lupe, Lupe. Forgive me, *chica*. You deserve better. And, really, what chance did we have? You've got Jesse, a job, a place in this world, and I'm still walking a tightrope where every time I fall, it's a mess.

I get all the way to the gate before my conscience catches up to me. Betting Lupe's money was my mistake. All she did was happen upon a crime in progress, and what kind of dog would I be if I stranded her here because of that? I'll lie to a liar, cheat a cheater, and rob a thief blind, but that's that world, not this one. In this one, I'm obligated to set things right. I'll admit what I did, scrounge up the money to pay her back double, then crawl away on my belly.

I turn and head back to the grandstand even though most of me still wants to run the other way.

THE FIRST PERSON I see when I get inside is Paul. He's hiding in a corner, watching hungrily as two drunks wave wads of money in each other's faces. That gun has obviously given him big ideas, and I suddenly get an idea of my own.

I sneak up behind him and bark, "Hands up!"

He whips around, frightened.

"Better be careful," he says when he sees it's me, then pats the bulge under his shirt.

"Loan me twenty dollars," I say.

"Go fuck yourself," he replies.

"Security!" I yell, not quite loud enough to be heard over the din but loud enough to spook Paul.

"What the hell?" he whispers.

"Give me a twenty," I say.

He hesitates, licking his lips while trying to decide if I'm bluffing. His hand is shaking when he finally passes me the money. He's angry, humiliated.

"I'll pay you back," I say.

"I'll pay *you* back," he says.

It could very well end that way, but I don't have time to worry about it now. I hurry to the betting windows, stopping only long enough to consult a tote for the current odds.

My Hail Mary is this: I take the twenty from Paul and put it with the four dollars I have left in my pocket and box four horses, the two, four, five, and seven, in a superfecta. If these horses come in first through fourth in any order in the next race, I'll win somewhere around a thousand bucks. It's like throwing your last dollar into a slot machine—a sucker's play—but it's the only chance I've got.

My phone rings.

"Where are you?" Lupe says.

"I ran into a couple buddies. I'll be up soon."

"But we're all alone."

"A few more minutes," I say.

"You better have my money," she snaps, then ends the call. My God, how many times has this girl been fucked over? I decide to hole up in the bathroom in case she comes looking for me. I find an empty stall and lock myself inside. At first I stand, facing the door, but that's too weird, so I cover the seat with toilet paper and sit down. My day began in jail, and now I'm trapped in a racetrack shitter. Somebody's made some bad choices. Again.

Talk to a shrink or a counselor or the folks at Gamblers Anonymous, and they'll give you all kinds of explanations for why you do it. They'll tell you that it's chemical, that you have a death wish, that you secretly want to lose in order to be punished for the sins of your past, that you're trying to return to a childlike state where miracles still happen.

It's a lot simpler for me: I gamble because I want to win. I like to win. It makes me feel good. And you need something to make you feel good after ten hours of loading trucks for some prick who thinks you're dirt, after sitting across the desk from a parole officer who's waiting for you to violate, after listening to your mom put you down again like she has your whole life. When I take a chump for twenty bucks on a pool table or pick up a few pots in a card game, something opens up inside me, and I'm as good as everyone else thinks they are—no, better. For an hour or a day, however long my streak lasts, every move I make is the right one, and my smile can bring the world to its knees. The only problem is, it can't last forever. You have to lose eventually so that someone else can win. Bitch and moan all you want, but that's the first, and worst, rule of the universe.

It stinks in the stall. I hold my nose, breathe through my mouth. Lupe calls again, and I let it go to voice mail. A text comes in a few seconds later: *Where the f r u?*

I'm going to lay off the ponies after this, stick to what I know best, eight ball and hold 'em. I'm going to get serious about getting serious: practice more, enter some tournaments, start acting like the pro I want to be. The jail thing was a stumble, not a fall. I'm still standing, still in it, still the only one who can bring me down.

The announcer's voice comes crackling over the PA. The race has started. I unlock the stall and run out to watch it on the nearest screen. The shouts of the spectators fill the cavern beneath the grandstand so that I can't hear the call, but three of my picks look to be in position coming out of the backstretch, and the final one is moving up.

My heart is pounding, and I set off at a run for the finish line. Skirting the crowds gathered under the monitors, I burst into the sunshine and fresh air and push my way up front where everybody is yelling *"Go! Go! Go!"* as the horses cross the line, my horses: seven, two, five, four. I pump my fist once, just once, and those aren't tears you see, you fucker. Those aren't tears.

I WAVE LUPE'S money over my head as I approach her and Jesse in the stands. "Hey, hey, hey," I say, doing a little dance. Lupe isn't having any of it. Her eyes are icy cold. She snatches her winnings out of my hand and tells Jesse to get up. He looks like he's been crying.

"Take us home," Lupe says.

"Whoa, now, at least give me a chance to explain," I say. Old friends, I tell her, guys from way back. One of them had gotten married; another's dad had died. I tried to get away, but you know how it is. Sometimes you have to hear a buddy out.

"I don't care if it was your mother you saw," she says. "Nobody treats me like that."

"Like what?" I say.

"Like a dumb bitch."

"Mom!" Jesse wails, upset by the swearing.

"I'm sorry, *mijo*," Lupe says. "I'm mad is all."

I thought she'd be happy to see me and her money, that the thrill of winning would do for her what it does for me: wipe away all the trouble it took to get there.

"Come on," I say. "I hit it big. Let's celebrate."

"Celebrate with yourself," she says.

It's a long, silent ride back to the valley. Jesse falls asleep in the backseat, and Lupe is busy texting, her hair hiding her face. I think about how excited I was this morning, looking forward to our date, and I wonder if there was ever any way it could have been what I wanted it to be.

By the time we get to the condo, the sun is sinking fast, dragging the day down with it. I say something that I hope will turn Lupe around and make her see the good in me, something that starts with "Please" and that I'd be ashamed for anybody else to hear, but she won't listen, won't even let me help her unload Jesse. I watch in the rearview mirror as she unbuckles the seat belt, slings the sleeping kid over her shoulder, and carries him to the lobby without looking back.

The streetlights come on as I'm driving to a bar I know with a hot backroom poker game. This normally gets my blood pumping, because I'm the kind of guy who does better at night than during the day. Night's when my people are out and about. Night's when the rules change in my favor. But right now I just feel sick. Sick of the hustle and the juke and the mask. I've got a pocketful of cash and luck running my way, but all I can think about is everything I've ever lost. And that's no good, man, no good at all, because if you sit down to play carrying that load, you're dead from the shuffle and cut.

GATHER DARKNESS

A TEXT COMES FROM Vince. All it says is *Cal and Esther,* and I have no idea what it means. Vince's messages are often cryptic like this. I assume it's because he wants to pique my interest in hope of receiving a response, but that doesn't make his coyness any less irritating.

I knew Cal and Esther at UCLA. We were friends, kind of, but lost touch after graduation. It's been years since I've seen them, long enough that they don't know about Julie, about Eve. Last I heard they'd gotten married. I think Vince still sees them now and then.

So? I text him back.

They're having a housewarming June 12. Boys' night out?

I think about it for a minute, then text *Sure* without consulting Julie first. She doesn't have to approve everything.

My nigga, Vince texts back.

My boss, Big Gay Bob, sticks his head into my office and asks if I saw the editorial about teacher layoffs in this morning's *Times*. I didn't, but I say I did.

"The councilman wants to respond," Bob says. "Give me something to run by him."

"Your wish is my command," I reply in a funny voice, then spin around to my computer like I'm going to get started right away. Instead, I sit there and pick a scab on my knuckle until it bleeds.

OUR CONDO HAS a small balcony that overlooks Wilshire Boulevard. The street is four lanes wide and noisy all the time. There's always a bus making a racket or a couple of Korean kids racing tricked-out Nissans. Still, the balcony is the only place I can be alone. Five floors above the Miracle Mile, facing south, the orange lights of the ghetto like a fire burning in the distance.

Julie and I have an arrangement: As soon as I walk in the door from work, I get a gin and tonic and a little time to decompress. Fifteen minutes on the balcony to myself, that's all I ask. After that I'm ready to be a good husband, to do the daddy thing.

Tonight that means letting Eve crawl all over me and tickle me with a big pink feather. She learned this from a cartoon, tickling someone with a feather. I pretend to laugh as she attacks the bottoms of my feet, my nose, my chin. When she sees how much fun I'm having, she gives me the feather and demands that I tickle her so she can pretend to laugh too.

"Don't rile her," Julie says. "Dinner's ready."

We've started saying grace before we eat because Julie wants Eve to have traditions.

"What are we, fucking Amish?" I said when she first came up with this.

"It's important," she said.

Julie and I grew up in regular families, families that ate dinner in front of the TV and talked about going to church on Christmas but somehow never made it. I used to fetch my dad beers from the fridge for quarter tips. The rules are different now. We're supposed to raise Eve to be one of those kids who weren't allowed to drink soda or play with toy guns, which is fine, I guess, if all the other kids are like that too. I want her to fit in. I want her to be happy.

I clean up the kitchen after we eat, load the dishwasher, and Julie gets Eve ready for bed. We tuck her in and kiss her good night together, then settle on the couch. Julie flips through a magazine while we watch our shows. Other nights she messes around on her iPad or works a crossword puzzle. What this means is that she's always so distracted that she can't follow the plot of even the dumbest sitcom.

"Who's he again?" she asks.

"The blond girl's uncle," I say.

My mind wanders too. I find myself thinking about little adventures I had as a kid, songs I used to be able to play on the guitar. My fingers twitch as I try to pick out the chords to "Under the Bridge." Julie laughs at me.

"What are you doing?" she says.

I feel fat sitting there on the couch with my wife in the watery light from the TV five stories above Wilshire Boulevard. Bloated. Like a greedy mosquito too full of blood to fly.

★   ★   ★

THE COUNCILMAN STOPS by the staff meeting to tell us what a great job we're doing. I write his press releases, help with his speeches, and take care of his website. He's okay. He's got more personality than brains, but what politician doesn't? He also has this way of talking down to you sometimes. He knows three things about me—that I went to UCLA, that I have a little girl, and that I sometimes eat Taco Bell for lunch—and that's enough for him. Every conversation we've ever had has revolved around one of those subjects.

Later we all gather in the break room for Maria the receptionist's birthday, cake and everything. I show up because you have to in a small office like this. I eat some ice cream and tell a funny story about Eve, but what I really want to talk about is what happened on my way to work this morning, that guy taking a shit in front of me.

I was waiting at a long red light, and a bum squatted on the grassy strip between the sidewalk and the street, dropped his pants, and let go. I tried to turn my head but couldn't. It was as if a bully had grabbed the back of my neck and was making me watch. I want to talk about how seeing that made me feel. Like everything was about to fall apart. Like pretty soon we'd all be shitting in the street.

The rest of the day slips away from me. I stare at the ceiling of my office mostly, at a water stain that looks like an octopus. My cell rings as I'm getting ready to go home. I don't recognize the number.

"Hello?" I say.

"This is Sophie."

My lungs seize up. I force a breath.

"Remember me?"

A couple of months ago Julie took Eve to her parents' place in Oxnard for the weekend. I stayed behind to catch up on some stuff, and Saturday night Vince and I went to dinner, had a few drinks. I felt pretty good driving back to the condo, a little drunk, a little high. The music on the radio was the perfect sound track for the movie I was in. The streetlights played their part, the cars, the buildings pulsing to the beat.

I passed a club I'd heard about, a place people went. Sometimes it hits you how long it's been since you had that kind of fun. I wasn't tired, nobody was waiting on me at home, so I turned around and parked. If there was a line or a cover charge—any kind of hassle at all—I was ready to leave, but I wound up breezing right in and even found a seat at the bar. It turned out to be next to this girl, Sophie, the one who's saying to me now, "We need to talk. And not on the phone."

THEY'RE SHOOTING SOMETHING around the corner, in one of the big houses in Hancock Park. Equipment trucks and portable dressing rooms line the street, and huge lights set up on the lawn stand in for the sun.

Julie and I are walking Eve, pushing her in her stroller. We go this way every Sunday morning, bring our coffee along. The kid waves at birds and has to pet all the friendly dogs we pass. Meanwhile, Julie plays games with her: Do you see a mailbox? Do you see a trash can? Sometimes I want to say, *Jesus, leave her alone.* She'll be in school soon enough, and people will pick her brain all day long.

Some guy with a walkie-talkie steps onto the sidewalk and blocks our way.

"Could I get you to cross the street?" he says.

"Why?" Julie says,

"We're filming here."

"So?"

"So you have to cross the street."

Julie's jaw tightens. She beat up a girl in junior high. The girl called her a slut, and Julie broke her nose. She's not proud of it, but she did it.

"We don't have to cross," she says. "You don't have any authority."

"Come on," the guy says. "Please."

Julie pushes the stroller toward him. He has to jump out of her way.

"Really?" he says as she rolls by.

I trail after her and give him a shrug and a smile.

We pass the cameras and craft services and a man holding a microphone on the end of a pole. A girl carrying a clipboard yells "Hey!" but Julie ignores her too. The rent-a-cop hired to stop traffic is lounging on his motorcycle. He gives us a sarcastic salute and chirps, "Thanks for your cooperation."

Julie fumes all the way into Larchmont Village. *Who do*

they think they are? We've got as much right to the sidewalk as they do. I quit listening when she starts talking about writing a letter to the newspaper. I haven't slept in two days, and it feels like bugs are crawling on my eyeballs.

"Do you see a fire engine?" I say to Eve. It's a test; there is no fire engine.

"There," Eve says. She points at a car driving by. The sky is milky white, and nothing has a shadow. Julie goes into the bakery for bread, and I wait outside with Eve. We watch an old man cross against the signal and someone in a silver Mercedes give him hell.

I SPEND THE morning drafting an op-ed piece on the redistricting proposal. The councilman is against it because the new map will put more Latinos in his area, and he's afraid they won't vote for a gringo. He can't come out and say that, of course, so he gave me a few useless notes and asked me to turn them into an acceptable counterargument.

Bob is breathing down my neck, but I can't build up any steam. Something's wrong with my chair. It's not quite right, like maybe the cleaning crew bumped the height knob over the weekend. I get down on my hands and knees three times to fiddle with it but keep making things worse.

My excuse for taking a long lunch is a doctor's appointment. Bob looks like he wants to squawk, but I tell him not to worry, I'll be back this afternoon and stay until I finish the piece. I drive into Hollywood and find the Starbucks where I'm meeting Sophie. It's in a shitty strip mall between a RadioShack and a Panda Express. I park in back, next to a padlocked dumpster.

I'm nervous walking in that I won't remember her. She had dark hair and dark eyes that I said something stupid about that night, how a man could get lost in them and never find his way home.

"Wow," she said. "The big guns already?"

That was the moment, me stammering and faking chagrin, her laughing and saying, "Just kidding." That was the last exit, and I sped past it. Even though it had been a while since I'd been out and about, since I'd done any flirting, I knew right then where we were headed.

Turns out she's easy to spot, the prettiest girl in the place. She's smaller than I recall, maybe older. She's wearing a white blouse and gray slacks, work clothes. She looks up from her phone as I approach, frowns, and I see the beauty mark on her upper lip, where I first kissed her.

"Should I sit?" I say.

"Sure," she replies.

The chair scrapes loudly across the floor as I pull it out. Everybody stares at us, our awkwardness palpable. I sit and put my hands in my lap, then on the table, then back in my lap.

She's pregnant.

Even if you're prepared for something like that, the actual words can still lay you out. I tilt my head back, close my eyes, and exhale through pursed lips.

"Okay," I say. "What do we do about it?"

"Don't worry," she scoffs. "I don't plan on being a

mommy right now, but the problem is, I don't have insurance."

This is one of the scenarios I've been playing out ever since I got her call, trying to be ready for anything.

"Whatever you need," I say.

"I need money," she says.

"How much?" I say.

She gazes past me, running numbers in her head. I find this charming. I would've already had a figure in mind.

"Fifteen hundred?" she says, as if asking if the amount is acceptable.

"All right," I say. "Give me a week."

My easy acquiescence seems to take her by surprise. Her eyes well up with tears, and I'm suddenly filled with tenderness toward her. I have to admit that for two seconds after we climbed out of the backseat of my car that night, after we kissed good-bye, I was in some kind of love with her. And in spite of all the guilt, remorse, and penitence that came later, the memory of her reaching up to pull me down on top of her is one I've often lingered over.

She shifts and sniffles and uses her napkin to wipe up a coffee spill on the table. Someone has etched a tag into the glass of the window behind her, and when the sun hits the scratches, they sparkle with a diamond's soulless brilliance.

"I guess I should have been more careful," she says. "But so should you."

"Absolutely," I say. "I totally blame myself."

"You're married?" she says, pointing at my ring.

"Yes," I say.

"Why weren't you wearing it that night?"

"I took it off."

She draws back her head and squints down her nose at me.

"That's fucked up," she says.

"I know," I say.

"It's disgusting."

I'm glad she's saying this. It's good for me. I need to hear what a rotten bastard I am because part of me still isn't convinced.

I realize I've had my sunglasses on since I got here. I reach up and take them off.

"Are you okay for now?" I say. "Do you need anything?"

"Give me twenty dollars," she says.

I reach for my wallet, slide the bill out.

"Wait," she says. "Give me forty. No, sixty. I don't even need it. I just want to take something from you."

"I only have forty," I say, and hand the money over.

A woman at the counter is trying to use a coupon to pay for her coffee. She gets loud when the cashier tells her it's expired, keeps asking the girl if she speaks English. I have to get back to the office.

"So, I'll text you," I say as I stand.

"Okay," Sophie says. She stands too.

"And I'll see you in a week. Here?"

"Here's good. I work close by."

We shake hands like it's business. I walk out the door, then think I'll get a coffee for the road. When I turn to go back inside, I see Sophie hugging some guy who'd been sitting at another table, watching us the whole time. Long hair, ponytail, beard. Her back is to me, but he and I lock eyes over her shoulder. I decide I don't need any coffee. I walk to my car, get in, and drive away.

On Tuesday, after we put Eve to bed, Julie asks me to go down with her to her car and help her carry up a new coffee table she bought at Ikea. We ride the elevator to the garage and pull the box out of the back of the Jetta. Julie takes one end, and I grab the other. The alarm on a Land Rover goes off as we pass by, and my guts jump. I don't like being down here with all that concrete and steel above me and the unquiet earth below.

"If you don't go slower, I'm going to drop it," Julie says.

I hold my finger on the call button until the elevator car arrives. The Land Rover's alarm is still echoing through the garage when the doors close.

We set the box down in the middle of the living room, and Julie opens one end and slides out the pieces of the table.

"Relax," I say. "I'll put it together."

"I want to do it," she says. "Read me the directions."

"Oh, boy," I say. "I better get another drink."

Julie frowns but doesn't reply. Her dad is a drunk, so she's touchy about booze. If I have more than the one G&T after work, she gets weird. Not to be rude, but she should mind her own fucking business.

I go into the kitchen and pour myself a tall one. Julie is already screwing stuff together when I return. I sit on the couch and, after consulting the assembly instructions, tell her what comes next.

"This can't be right," she says at one point.

I lean over to show her the diagram. "You have to turn that end around," I say.

"Yuck," she says, waving a hand in front of her face. "You stink."

It won't be difficult to sneak the money for Sophie out of our account. When we were first married, Julie ran the household, paying the bills and overseeing our finances, but when Eve was born, she asked me to take over. Now, as long as the ATM spits out cash when she sticks her card in, she's happy.

And that wasn't the only change the baby brought about. Julie was a loan officer when I met her, at a bank in Beverly Hills, and she kept working right up until she had Eve. She never complained, seemed to enjoy the job even, so I was shocked when she told me that she didn't plan to go back.

"I only want to be a wife and mother," she said. "My mom worked, and I always felt slighted. I want to devote myself to you and Eve."

I went from one life to another in just one year. I hooked up with Julie; she got pregnant three months later; we married, bought the condo, and had Eve. Truthfully, I was a bit disoriented, but when I tried to talk to Julie about it, she came on strong about my having to accept my new responsibilities the way she had to accept hers.

"I don't feel like I had much choice is all," I said.

"Sometimes adults don't get much choice," she said.

She tightens the last screw and flips the completed table right-side up.

"Ta-da."

I help her move the old table into the hallway and position the new one in front of the couch. We didn't need a new table, she just got bored with the old one. That's the kind of people we are now.

She picks up my empty glass, takes it into the kitchen, rinses it, and puts it into the dishwasher.

"I'm going to read in bed for a while," she says.

"I want to watch the news," I say.

I wait for her to close the bedroom door, then go into the kitchen, get a fresh glass from the cupboard, and make another drink. It's nice out on the balcony, warm, but with a breeze coming off the ocean. I stand with my forearms on the rail and watch the traffic. A car cruises past with its windows down, radio blaring. You can hear the kids inside singing along to whatever song is playing.

Have fun, boys and girls, I think. *Let this be the best night of your lives.*

VINCE CALLS ME at work, wants to know if I'm still on for Cal and Esther's party.

"Why wouldn't I be?" I reply, wondering if he knows something. I've been paranoid since meeting Sophie at Starbucks. That guy she was with made me uneasy.

"Come on," Vince says. "You flake all the time."

It's true. I say yes on Monday, but when Friday rolls around I'm so beat that all I want to do is stumble home and coast through the weekend on routine.

"I'm going, I'm going, I swear," I say. I lean back in my chair and pick up a photo of me and Julie and Eve at Christmas. It could be a picture of anybody. I don't even remember Christmas.

"Do you know any jokes?" Vince says.

"Jokes?"

"The dude in the mailroom here tells me a joke every day, and I thought I'd tell him one back, freak him out. I looked online, but they're all about having sex with babies and sick shit like that."

"That'd freak him out for sure."

"Yeah, and also get me fired."

Vince has been married to Kaylee for two years, and they were together for three before that. They're putting off having a kid because they want to travel. They went to Machu Picchu last year, and Vietnam is next. Julie doesn't like Kaylee; she says she needs to grow up. Vince, though, he loves her. He started crying one time telling me how much. We were in a bar, having some beers, and all this love came pouring out of him. I hoped he couldn't see how uncomfortable it made me.

"I have to go," I say into the phone.

"Knock-knock," Vince says.

"Who's there?"

"9/11."

"9/11 who?"

"Hey, you said you'd never forget."

The octopus on the ceiling is getting bigger, expanding like an incriminating bloodstain. I should call building maintenance about it. There may be a leak somewhere.

On my way home on Friday I pass by the spot where that bum shit on the grass, and I think that if I see him again, I'll kill him. An instant later I'm like, *What the fuck is wrong with you? Where did that come from?* It must have been a misfire or crossed wires. Or maybe it was somebody else speaking through me, maybe everybody else, the whole city.

Julie asked me to pick up a pizza at Scalo's. I place the order and get a beer for the wait. It's mostly a take-out and delivery joint, and I'm the only customer. I sit at a table in front of the window. The gas station on the corner is a mess. Cars are backed up into the street, trying to get to the pumps. And this is a regular day. What if something really goes wrong?

A girl running past the window startles me. She pushes on the door to Scalo's once, twice, again, until the guys behind the counter all yell "Pull!" at once. Stepping quickly into the restaurant, she turns and presses her face to the glass and looks back up the street in the direction she came from.

"You have bathroom?" she asks breathlessly, with some kind of accent.

"For customers only," Joseph, the owner, says.

The girl grimaces in disgust. She's nineteen, twenty, Russian, Iranian, something. Her mascara is smeared like she's been crying, and she keeps wiping at her nose. She gathers her bleached-blond hair in one hand and uses an elastic band that she takes from her pocket to make a ponytail, all the while staring out the window.

I swivel to follow her gaze, fighting the urge to duck. You've got all these guns and all these hotheads, guys who don't care who gets in the way when they lose it. But the only person I see is an old woman waiting at a bus stop half a block away.

"What's going on?" Joseph says.

The girl whips off her jacket, turns it inside out—from white to black—and slips it back on. She opens the door and sticks her head out for a better view of the street.

"You want me to call the police?" Joseph says.

The girl disappears, is suddenly gone, running again.

Joseph shakes his head.

"Gypsies," he says to me.

I nod like I know and sip my beer. But I don't know anything. Joseph is from Lebanon. His brother was killed by a sniper one morning while walking home from the store with a loaf of bread and some eggs. His father was blown to pieces by a rocket.

"They are both making a long vacation, beautiful holidays," he said to me once. "That is what I tell myself to keep from going crazy."

★   ★   ★

CAL AND ESTHER live out in Highland Park, a neighborhood that used to be mostly working-class Latinos but is now filling up with young white couples who want affordable houses and yards for their dogs. Vince says he'll drive. We take freeways and streets I've never heard of to get there, and when we do, taco stands and pawnshops alternate with art galleries and cupcake bakeries. It's confusing.

The house is a tiny stucco box on a street lined with the kind of big, old trees you rarely see in L.A. Elms and things. We park down the block in front of a duplex with a Tinker Bell bounce house set up in the yard. Mexican music blares out of a pair of speakers in the bed of a pickup parked at the curb, and dozens of kids dart about in unison like flocking birds.

"That's the party we should be going to," Vince says. "Teach them youngsters how to do the ice cream and cake and cake."

A sign on the front door of Cal and Esther's house directs guests to the backyard. Music and the sound of voices grow louder as we pass through a gate in the wooden fence and walk down a narrow passage past the garbage cans and a wheelbarrow. We brush by a guy smoking in the shadows and pop out into the party, and I'm glad to see there's a crowd. I worried we'd be the only ones.

The yard is much larger than the house, with a covered patio and a vegetable garden. Candy-colored Christmas lights are twined through the branches of the lemon trees and dangle from the eaves of a toolshed. I brought a bottle of wine as a gift for Cal and Esther, and Vince got them a book on home repairs. A girl Vince knows but I don't shows us where to put them and points us toward the bar, which is set up on a picnic table.

Vince pumps the keg while I pour some Maker's over ice. Cal appears out of the crowd. He has a beard now. He greets Vince with a slap on the back and picks up a corkscrew.

"How's tricks?" I say to him.

His smile flickers, and he squints like he's having trouble placing me.

"Danny?" he says.

He must be joking. We worked at the campus library together, took mushrooms in Disneyland with a bunch of people, went to Radiohead. He knows who I am.

"I heard you and Esther got married," I say. "Congratulations."

"Thanks," he says, then looks past me. "Hey, Esther," he calls out. "Did you see who's here?"

"Oh my God," she says and comes over to join us. I can tell she also has only a vague recollection of who I am, and I feel as if I'm disappearing from the past and the present at the same time, like an old photograph in which the people have faded into ghostly blurs. It's not right. These two weren't special enough to have forgotten me.

I tell them about Julie and Eve and my job, making everything sound better than it is. They nod and smile and say, "That's great," but they're only being polite. Cal makes his escape first, then Esther, tossing "Keep in touch" over her shoulder as she walks away.

I finish my bourbon and pour myself another and decide to hide out in the bathroom. There are two women with babies in the kitchen. I tell them where I want to go, and they point me down the hall.

I lock myself in and sit on the edge of the tub with my head in my hands. After a while I get up and check the medicine cabinet and pocket a bottle of Xanax prescribed for Cal. Someone knocks, and I pretend to wash my hands, then let the girl in.

A handwritten sign on a door at the end of the hall catches my eye: *Keep Out.* I open the door and find myself in Cal and Esther's bedroom. The walls are painted a funny color, like everyone was doing a few years ago, and a big blowup of that famous photo of a couple kissing in Paris hangs over the bed.

I walk to the dresser and lift the lid of a jewelry box sitting on top. I pick one pearl earring out of all the junk and hope Esther will go crazy trying to figure out where it went when she wants to wear it someday.

The door opens, and Cal is standing there, looking confused. "Hey," he says. "This room is kind of off-limits."

"Sorry," I say. "There was someone in the bathroom, so I was looking for another."

"There's only one," he says. "You'll have to wait."

I flush the earring down the toilet when I get into the bathroom again, then go out and tell Vince I'm not feeling well. And it's true. I roll down the window and let the wind blow in my face as we race down the freeway, but no matter how much air I gulp, it isn't enough. I want to turn myself inside out and shake myself clean. I want to sleep for years and wake with this life behind me.

THE CEILING OF my office collapses over the weekend. I come in on Monday morning to find the soggy panels lying on my desk and chair, and dirty water soaking the carpet. A broken pipe, the man from building maintenance says.

"You didn't notice anything?" he asks.

"Nope," I say, not mentioning the octopus.

Juan the IT guy moves my computer to an empty desk in a cubicle in the hall so I can keep working while they do repairs. I spend most of the morning updating the website, but people keep poking their heads in to ask what happened.

The councilman himself stops by around noon. He and Bob are just back from a press conference where the police announced the capture of some nut who'd been setting cars on fire in the district. The councilman is exuberant. He loves being in front of the cameras.

"I hear the sky is falling," he says.

"It's not a big deal," I say. "They should be done fixing everything by three."

"Good, good. You going to Taco Bell for lunch?"

"Maybe."

He pulls a twenty out of his pocket.

"I saw a commercial for a new thing there," he says. "The Beefy Crunch Burrito or something. Would you mind bringing me one back?"

"No," I say. "Sure."

He hands me the money.

"Get yourself one too, or whatever you want," he says.

He's talking down to me again, but that's okay. He'll be shitting in the streets with the rest of us soon enough.

Sophie is sitting at the same table she was last week, and that guy is there too, hunched over his phone in the corner by the window. He glances at me when I come in, then quickly looks away. I give Sophie a little wave and sit down across from her. She's dressed for work again, her hair pulled back. A tiny gold crucifix hangs around her neck. I didn't notice it last time, or that night at the club either.

"How are you?" I say.

"Fine," she says.

"Everything okay?"

"Super-duper."

I wasn't going to say what I say next. I'd decided to ignore my suspicions and give her the money even after I looked it up and found out that an abortion only costs five hundred dollars. It's a nasty procedure, and I was willing to throw in the extra for pain and suffering. She had to bring that guy, though. If it was just her, okay, but something about him sets me off.

So I say it.

"You wouldn't have any proof, would you?"

"Proof of what?" Sophie says.

"That you're pregnant," I say.

Sophie's expression doesn't change as she reaches into her purse and pulls out a folded sheet of paper and hands it to me.

"I was wondering why you didn't ask last time," she says.

It's a letter on stationery from a women's health-care center stating that Sophie Ricard is pregnant and has a due date of February 11 next year. I pass her the envelope containing the money, but I'm still not satisfied. I'm still disappointed in her.

I point at the long-haired guy, who's glaring at me like he'd like to tear my head off.

"Is that your boyfriend?" I ask Sophie.

"What's it to you?" she says.

"How do I know it's not his baby?" I say.

She slides the envelope into her purse.

"That's right," she snaps. "How do you know?"

I stand and walk out without saying another word. I plan to leave with an angry squeal of rubber, but my car is parked in the sun, and I have to sit with the air conditioner on until the steering wheel cools enough for me to drive away.

HERE'S HOW I'M going to think about it: *You dodged a bullet; be grateful.* And if I ever tell anybody the story, I'm going to say that the experience made me a better husband and father. I lift my gin and tonic to affirm this, salute the setting sun, the traffic roaring by, the ghetto simmering on the horizon.

The slider opens behind me, and Julie sticks her head out.

"Dinner's ready," she says.

We're eating early tonight. She's going to a movie with someone, a friend.

"I'm coming," I say.

She leaves the door open. I set my glass on the railing of the balcony and shake my hand like it's numb. Then I reach out and give the glass a nudge with my index finger, and another nudge, and another, until it falls. I lean over the railing and watch the glass shatter on the sidewalk below. Man, that was dumb, wasn't it? I could've hurt somebody.

"Daddy."

Eve comes onto the balcony through the open door. I pick her up and hold her at arm's length.

"You know the rules," I say. "You're not supposed to be out here. It's dangerous."

"It's time to eat," she says.

"All right," I say.

We step to the railing, a man and a child—no, a father and his daughter. I show her the view.

"Do you see a helicopter?" I say.

"Mmm, no," she says,

"Do you see a car?"

"There."

She points down at the traffic on Wilshire.

The dark inside me begins to bray, and I fight back as best I can. "We're going to be okay," I say, "we're going to be great," but I can barely hear myself over the din.

INSTINCTIVE
DROWNING RESPONSE

MARYROSE DIES ON WEDNESDAY, and on Friday Campbell dreams he was there when it happened. Tony said she passed out right after she fixed, slumped over on the couch, so that's where that part comes from. And then Tony stuck her in the shower to try to revive her, and that part's there too. In the dream, however, Campbell is with them, and Maryrose's eyes pop open as soon as the cold water hits her, and she shakes her head and yells, "What the fuck's going on?" "Nothing, baby, nothing," Campbell replies, and—it's a dream, remember—they live happily ever after. But dreams are bullshit. Dreams break your heart. When someone's dead, she's dead, and when it's someone you loved, some of your world dies with her. The places Campbell went with Maryrose give him the creeps now. Everything that used to be fun isn't anymore. He can't bring himself to sit on their favorite bench in the park, and the tacos at Siete Mares taste like dirt. At least dope still does him right. Thank God for dope.

★   ★   ★

THEY MET AT a cemetery called Hollywood Forever where movies were shown in the summer. Friends of his and friends of hers brought blankets and Spanish cheese and splurgy bottles of wine, and everybody sprawled on the grass to stare at Clint Eastwood in a cowboy hat projected onto the wall of a mausoleum. Campbell got up to have a cigarette after the big shootout, and Maryrose asked if she could bum one. They smoked together under a palm tree and made fun of themselves for being degenerates. Somehow they got on the subject of drugs. It was kind of a game. Ever done this? Ever done that? Maryrose surprised Campbell when she said yes to junk. "That shit'll kill you," he said. "Well, yeah," she said. "Someday." A week later he moved into her place in Silver Lake. He hadn't had a craft services gig in over a month and working the door at Little Joy paid mostly in drinks. Maryrose told him not to worry about it because her dad took care of the rent. The apartment overlooked a storefront church, the kind with a hand-painted sign and a couple of rows of battered folding chairs. Services started every night at seven. *"O Dios, por tu nombre, sálvame,"* the preacher would shout. *"O precioso sangre de Jesús."* Maryrose liked to get stoned and lie in front of the open window and listen to the congregation send their hymns up to heaven. "It's so beautiful," she'd groan, tears as hot and bright as stars streaming down her cheeks.

★   ★   ★

Campbell cops for Martin now and then, and Martin hires Campbell to help him and his brothers serve food to film crews on location. They're downtown today, where a sci-fi thing is shooting, and Campbell is handing out lattes and doughnuts to little green men and robot soldiers. He watches a couple of extras flirt and tries to see it as the sweet start of something but isn't feeling expansive enough yet. Since Maryrose died, anything not rimed with sorrow is suspect; anything gentle, anything hopeful, is as deceptive as a thirteen-year-old girl's daydream of love, a sugarcoated time bomb. Martin brings over one of the actors. He introduces him as Doc, but Campbell knows his real name, everybody does, he's that famous. "Doc likes to party," Martin says, and everybody knows what that means too. "Can you hook him up?" An explosion goes off on the set. Campbell and Martin and Doc all jump and giggle, and Doc points out a flock of startled pigeons wheeling overhead, scared shitless.

Maryrose dies on Wednesday, and a week later her mother and sister show up at the apartment and kick Campbell out. He feels like a criminal, packing his stuff, the way they watch him to make sure he doesn't take anything of Maryrose's. "I blame you," her mother says. "And I hope the weight of that crushes you." He calls his own mother for money. She says no, and his dad doesn't even answer the phone. They hope he gets crushed too, but they call it "tough love." Tony lets him stay at his house, the same house where Maryrose OD'd. At night, from his bed in the spare room, Campbell hears Tony telling the story over and over to his customers. "She was gone, dude, just like that." To pay his way he makes deliveries for Tony, drives him around, washes his dishes, and takes out his trash. Then they get high and watch tattoo shows on TV. Tony is covered with tattoos, even has one with some of his dead mother's ashes mixed into the ink. "You know, she thought you were an idiot," Campbell says one night when Tony's so fucked up that he's drooling. "Who?" Tony says. "Maryrose," Campbell says. Tony nods for a second like he's thinking this over, then says again, "Who?"

SHE'D DROPPED OUT of USC, dropped out of Art Center and dropped out of the Fashion Institute, and the six months her parents had given her to decide what she wanted to do with her life were almost up. If she wasn't back in school by September, they'd cut her off. Some days she was defiant, shouting, "I'm proud to be a traitor to my class!" Other days she was too depressed to get out of bed. She'd stream sitcoms from her childhood, the laugh tracks taunting her as she buried her head under her pillow. Campbell worried about her when she was like this. He asked other girls he knew for advice. "She needs a project," one of them said, so he bought her some clay. They sat together in the breakfast nook and made a mess sculpting little pigs and turtles and snakes. "You're really good at this," Campbell told her. The scorn that flashed across her face let him know she'd seen through him. She smashed the giraffe she'd been working on and locked herself in the bathroom with their last bindle of Mexican brown.

Doc was a lifeguard before he was a movie star, and that's what he talks about when Campbell shows up at his house in Laurel Canyon with the dope he ordered. Martin is there too, and the three of them sit out on the deck, drinking beer and trying to pretend heroin isn't the only thing they have in common. "When someone is super close to drowning, they don't struggle or scream or splash," Doc says. "What happens is, their mind shuts off and pure instinct takes over. They can't cry for help, they can't wave their arms, they can't even grab a rope if you throw them one, because they're totally focused on one thing: keeping their head above water and taking their next breath. What it looks like is climbing a ladder, like they're trying to climb a ladder in the water, and if you don't reach them within twenty or thirty seconds, they're goners." Doc smokes his junk because he doesn't want marks, but he watches intently while Campbell and Martin fix. Afterward, Campbell lies on a chaise lounge and listens to the sounds of a party going on somewhere down-canyon, music and laughter riding on the back of a desert wind. He remembers a line from a book about Charles Manson, about how on the night of the Tate murders, which took place in another canyon not far from here, the same wind made it possible to hear ice cubes clinking a mile away. All of a sudden he's uneasy, imagining a gang of acid-crazed hippies sneaking up on them. He stands and walks to the railing, his heart tossing in his chest, and scans the hillside below the house for an escape route. A coyote trail criss-crosses the slope like a nasty scar, and if he needed to, he could scramble down it to the road and be the lucky one who gets away.

MARYROSE DIES ON Wednesday, and Campbell finds out about it a couple of hours later, when Tony calls him at the bar. During the conversation Campbell goes from staring at some LMU chick's fake ID to sitting on the sidewalk. He slaps away any helping hands and shuts his ears to all consolation. His and Maryrose's thing was them against the world, and to let anyone in now would be a betrayal. He keeps waiting to cry but never does. The ground doesn't open up, the moon stays where it is in the sky. When his legs work again, he gets up and walks. Straight down Sunset toward the ocean. He crosses PCH early the next morning and collapses on the sand. The fog is so thick he can't see the waves, only hear them pounding the shore. Good. Nothing. Anymore. Ever. The cops show up later that day, after he's ridden the bus back to the apartment. The detective who does the talking is a tall woman with white, white teeth. Campbell answers all her questions with lies. He doesn't do dope, Maryrose didn't do dope, and Tony is a fucking saint. The woman and her partner move gingerly around the place, like they're afraid to touch anything, and when Campbell coughs, the woman winces and claps a protective hand over her nose.

THEY TALKED ABOUT getting a dog, even went to the shelter to look for one. All they found there were psychotic pit bulls and shivering Chihuahuas, and the smell and the barking drove them out after just a few minutes. "Are you telling me normal people can deal with that?" Maryrose said. She liked to cook but forgot pots on the stove, left them simmering until the smoke alarm went off. Driving too. She'd wrecked a couple of cars, and the one she had when Campbell met her bore the dents and scrapes of a dozen close calls, a hundred little lapses, each a new wound to lick. When she was straight she wanted to be what she wasn't: productive and reliable, focused and stable. "Some people are just made messy," Campbell told her. "Not me," she replied. "I was born right and got twisted." Whole days went by like that, where he couldn't crack her codes. When she was happy, though, when she was high, contentment oozed from her like sweet-smelling sap. She'd name the ducks in Echo Park, dance to the music of the ice cream truck, and press her lips to his throat and leave them there. When she was happy, when she was high.

DOC STARTS TEXTING Campbell at all hours, stuff like *Hey, man* and *Ragin' tonight?* What it boils down to is he wants dope. Campbell tries to blow him off in the beginning, because dealing to a movie star seems like a good way to get busted, but then his own habit gets out of hand, and he has no money, and Doc pays double for everything and doesn't like to party alone. Campbell spends one night at the guy's house, a couple more the next week, and then he's practically living there. They sleep all day and order in from expensive restaurants. Doc's name is magic. A chef from one of the places actually delivers the food himself and puts the finishing touches on the meal in the house's kitchen. The girls who drop by every now and then aren't whores, but they'll take whatever they can get. Tall, leggy creatures, they know how to sit in short dresses and run in high heels, and all their conversations are in another language about some other world. Doc is always relieved when they leave for their parties and clubs, when it's finally just him and Campbell and the dope comes out.

One day they drive down to the Strip to eat lunch. Afterward a display of sunglasses in the window of a store catches Doc's eye. He goes inside and tries on a few pairs and makes Campbell try some too, sharing a mirror with him. "Those are hot on you," he says about one pair. "Like Michael Pitt hot." He insists on buying them for Campbell. Seven-hundred-dollar sunglasses. Campbell wears them later that afternoon when he makes a quick trip to the east side to replenish their stash. The bums look jaunty through the perfectly tinted lenses, the poor Mexicans happy. "How much do you think these cost?" Campbell asks Tony. "What the fuck do I care?" Tony replies. The sun is going down on his way back to the canyon, shining through the windshield at an annoying angle. With his new glasses he can stare right into it and take all the glare it has to give.

MARYROSE DIES ON Wednesday. There's a funeral two weeks later, but Campbell isn't invited. He moves out of Tony's and in with a bartender from Little Joy. Everything is good until the guy finds blood spattered on the bathroom wall and a syringe under the couch and tells Campbell to pack his shit and go. "I've lived with junkies before," he says. "They're nothing but holes that can't be filled. And they steal." So it's back to Tony's, back to the house where Maryrose died. He continues to shoot up on the couch where she shot up and to shower in the tub where her heart stopped beating. It's a curse, having to relive the worst over and over, trying to breathe that air, and he knows that if he doesn't get away, he's going to die too.

The first step is to retake the reins of his habit, be a man about it. Without too much suffering he manages to taper off to two hits a day. What eventually derails him is some punk at the bar who knew Maryrose saying something stupid about "that's what happens when an angel dances with the devil" and then, later, a photo he happens upon while scrolling through the pictures on his phone. It's Maryrose the day before she OD'd, looking like a ghost already. And he's the one who did that to her. She was just chipping when they met, and trying to keep up with him is what got her hooked. It's not a new realization, but this time it hurts enough to serve as a reason for backsliding into a three-day bender that hollows out his head and scrapes his bones clean of flesh. *Oh, baby,* he thinks when he finally pops to the surface on a bright fall morning when the tree shadows look like claws grabbing at the sidewalk, *I can't come meet you there ever again.*

HE AND MARYROSE tried to kick together after a bad balloon of what was supposed to be tar burned going in and made them both vomit their souls into the kitchen sink. This even after they'd been warned not to buy from that dealer by someone whose brother had ended up in the hospital just from smoking the stuff. If they were so strung out they'd risk shooting rat poison, it was time to quit. They threw some clothes into a suitcase, gassed up Campbell's Toyota, and headed out into the desert. Traffic on the freeway inched along, and the city stretched on forever. They stopped for lunch at Del Taco, but neither of them could eat. Then the army of windmills near Palm Springs freaked Maryrose out, the relentless turning of their giant blades suggesting an inexorability that was at odds with her lace-winged fantasy of bucking her fate. They checked into a desiccated motel on the shore of the Salton Sea. Even though the thermometer outside the office read 100 degrees, Maryrose wanted to walk down to the beach. It was covered with fish bones and scavenging gulls and had a stench that stuck in their throats. Back in the room they turned the noisy air conditioner to high and shivered under the thin blanket, unable to decide if they were hot or cold. Maryrose clutched her cramping stomach and kicked her feet. "My legs," she moaned. "My legs." She sat up, lay down, and sat up again. Gritting his teeth against his own agony, Campbell limped into the bathroom and drew her a glass of water. She drank it down but immediately vomited onto the linoleum next to the bed. Campbell placed his hand on her burning forehead and tried to mumbo jumbo some of her pain into him. He finally passed out for a while, waking near dawn.

They dragged themselves out to the car as soon as the sun bubbled red on the horizon and turned back toward L.A. Tony was still up from the night before. He sold them some shit, and they fixed right then and there, marveling at how fine they suddenly felt. They never discussed the trip as a failure, only joked about what fools they'd been for thinking they could go cold turkey. Vague plans were floated to try to kick again in a month or so, this time with some Xanax or Klonopin to help with the withdrawals, but they always found some reason to put it off.

Aww, DAMN, HERE they come up the drive: Doc's agent, Doc's manager, and Doc's little brother, to serve as muscle. "Shoot me up quick," Doc demands, thrusting out his arm. Campbell ignores him, more worried about gathering his belongings before he gets the bum's rush. He's hurrying up the stairs when they come through the door. Doc yells at them to keep the fuck away and let him be, but Campbell can hear in his voice that he's ready to get off the roller coaster. Doc's brother busts in on Campbell as he's stuffing his clothes into his backpack. "If you're not out of here in two minutes, I'm calling the cops," the brother says. When Campbell walks past him, he shoves Campbell toward the stairs, almost knocking him down. "Touch me again, and I'll sue," Campbell says. "You're not suing any-body, you fucking loser," the brother scoffs. Doc is sitting on the sofa between his manager and his agent. He's crying like a scared little boy, and his manager is stroking his hair and telling him everything will be fine. His brother stays on Campbell's tail all the way out to the driveway. Campbell hops into his car and wills it to start on the first try. The rear window shatters as he reaches the street, making him flinch and slam on the brakes. Doc's brother drops the other rock he's holding and dares Campbell to make something of it. That very evening Campbell trades the fancy sunglasses for fifty dollars' worth of junk.

MARYROSE DIES ON Wednesday, and a year—a year!—later Campbell marks the anniversary by returning to Echo Park, which he's been avoiding since her passing. He's a month sober, going to meetings, but struggles every day. Martin quit too, Tony's in jail, and Doc did a very public stint in rehab and emerged a hero. Campbell tosses some potato chips to the ducks, but not one of them has the energy to climb out of the water and waddle up the bank to get them. It's the third day of a heat wave, and the sun is showing everyone who's boss. Grass crumbles underfoot, palms hiss overhead, and the forsaken stand in the shadows of telephone poles, waiting for buses that are always late.

Maryrose claimed that the first time she did dope was the first time in her life she felt normal. "Why do you think it's called a fix?" she said. Campbell didn't argue; he just liked to see her smile. They'd come down to this bench, eat *paletas,* and make up songs about the people passing by. She'd laugh herself silly crooning about a fat kid kicking a soccer ball, then collapse breathless into his arms. And that's when *he* felt normal for the first time. But who's going to believe that? Who even wants to hear it? Better to keep those memories to himself, to guard them like a treasure against time, the goddamn drip, drip, drip of days that would wash them away.

APOCRYPHA

IF I HAD MONEY, I'd go to Mexico. Not Tijuana or Ensenada, but farther down, *real* Mexico. Get my ass out of L.A. There was this guy in the army, Marcos, who was from a little town on the coast called Mazunte. He said you could live pretty good there for practically nothing. Tacos were fifty cents, beers a buck.

"How do they feel about black folks?" I asked him.

"They don't care about anything but the color of your money," he said.

I already know how to speak enough Spanish to get by, how to ask for things and order food. *Por favor* and *muchas gracias*. The numbers to a hundred.

THE CHINESE FAMILY across the hall are always cooking in their room. I told Papa-san to cut it out, but he just stood there nodding and smiling with his little boy and little girl wrapped around his legs. The next day I saw Mama-san coming up the stairs with another bag of groceries, and this morning the whole floor smells like deep-fried fish heads again. I'm not an unreasonable man. I ignore that there are four of them living in a room meant for two, and I put up with the kids playing in the hall when I'm trying to sleep, but I'm not going to let them torch the building.

I pull on some pants and head downstairs. The elevator is broken, so it's four flights on foot. The elevator's always broken, or the toilet, or the sink. Roaches like you wouldn't believe too. The hotel was built in 1928, and nobody's done anything to it since. Why should they? There's just a bunch of poor people living here, Chinamen and wetbacks, dope fiends and drunks. Hell, I'm sure the men with the money are on their knees every night praying this heap falls down so they can collect on the insurance and put up something new.

The first person I see when I hit the lobby—the first person who sees *me*—is Alan. I call him Youngblood. He's the boy who sweeps the floors and hoses off the sidewalk.

"Hey, B, morning, B," he says, bouncing off the couch and coming at me. "Gimme a dollar, man. I'm hungry as a motherfucker."

I raise my hand to shut him up, walk right past him. I don't have time for his hustle today.

"They're cooking up there again," I say to the man at the desk, yell at him through the bulletproof glass. He's Chinese too, and every month so are more of the tenants. I know what's going on, don't think I don't.

"Okay, I talk to them," the man says, barely looking up from his phone.

"It's a safety hazard," I say.

"Yeah, yeah, okay," he says.

"Yeah, yeah, okay to you," I say. "Next time I'm calling the fire department."

Youngblood is waiting for me when I finish. He's so skinny he uses one hand to hold up his jeans when he walks. Got lint in his hair, boogers in the corners of his eyes, and he smells like he hasn't bathed in a week. That's what dope'll do to you.

"Come on, B, slide me a dollar, and I'll give you this," he says.

He holds out his hand. There's a little silver disk in his palm, smaller than a dime.

"What is it?" I say.

"It's a battery, for a watch."

"And what am I supposed to do with it?"

"Come on, B, be cool."

Right then the front door opens, and three dudes come gliding in, the light so bright behind them they look like they're stepping out of the sun. I know two of them: J Bone, who stays down the hall from me, and his homeboy Dallas. A couple of grown-up crack babies, crazy as hell. The third one, the tall, good-looking kid in the suit and shiny shoes, is a stranger. He has an air about him like he doesn't belong down here, like he ought to be pulling that suitcase through an airport in Vegas or Miami. He moves and laughs like a high roller, a player, the kind of brother you feel good just standing next to.

He and his boys walk across the lobby, goofing on one

another. When they get to the stairs, the player stops and says, "You mean I got to carry my shit up four floors?"

"I'll get it for you," J Bone says. "No problem."

The Chinaman at the desk buzzes them through the gate, and up they go, their boisterousness lingering for a minute like a pretty girl's perfume.

"Who was that?" I say, mostly to myself.

"That's J Bone's cousin," Youngblood says. "Fresh outta County."

No, it's not. It's trouble. Come looking for me again.

THE OLD MAN asks if I know anything about computers. He's sitting in his office in back, jabbing at the keys of the laptop his son bought him to use for inventory but that the old man mainly plays solitaire on. He picks the thing up and sets it down hard on his desk as if trying to smack some sense into it.

"Everything's stuck," he says.

"Can't help you there, boss," I say. "I was out of school before they started teaching that stuff."

I'm up front in the showroom. I've been the security guard here for six years now, ten to six, Tuesday through Saturday. Just me and the old man, day after day, killing time in the smallest jewelry store in the district, where he's lucky to buzz in ten customers a week. If I was eighty-two years old and had his money, I wouldn't be running out my string here, but his wife's dead, and his friends have moved away, and the world keeps changing so fast that I guess this is all he has left to anchor him, his trade, the last thing he knows by heart.

I get up out of my chair—he doesn't care if I sit when nobody's in the store—and tuck in my uniform. Every so often I like to stretch my legs with a stroll around the showroom. The old man keeps the display cases looking nice, dusts the rings and bracelets and watches every day, wipes down the glass. I test him now and then by leaving a thumbprint somewhere, and it's always gone the next morning.

Another game I play to pass the time, I'll watch the people walking by outside and bet myself whether the next one'll be black or Mexican, a man or a woman, wearing a hat or not, things like that. Or I'll lean my chair back as far as it'll go, see how long I can balance on the rear legs. The old man doesn't like that one, always yells, "Stop fidgeting. You make me nervous." And I've also learned to kind of sleep with my eyes open and my head up, half in this world, half in the other.

I walk over to the door and look outside. It's a hot day, and folks are keeping to the shade where they can. Some are waiting for a bus across the street, in front of the music store that blasts that *oom pah pah oom pah pah* all day long. Next to that's a McDonald's, then a bridal shop, then a big jewelry store with signs in the windows saying *Compramos Oro, We Buy Gold.*

A kid ducks into our doorway to get out of the sun. He's yelling into his phone in Spanish and doesn't see me standing on the other side of the glass, close enough I can count the pimples on his chin.

"¿Por qué?" he says. That's "Why?" or sometimes "Because." "¿Por qué? ¿Por qué?"

When he feels my eyes on him, he flinches, startled. I chuckle as he moves out to the curb. He glances over his shoulder a couple times like I'm something he's still not sure of.

"Is it too cold in here?" the old man shouts.

He's short already, but hunched over like he is these days, he's practically a midget. Got about ten hairs left on his head, all white, ears as big as a goddamn monkey's, and those kind of thick glasses that make your eyes look like they belong to someone else.

"You want me to dial it down?" I say.

"What about you? Are you cold?" he says.

"Don't worry about me," I say.

Irving Mandelbaum. I call him Mr. M or boss. He's taken to using a cane lately, if he's going any distance, and I had to call 911 a while back when I found him facedown on the office floor. It was just a fainting spell, but I still worry.

"Five degrees, then," he says. "If you don't mind."

I adjust the thermostat and return to my chair. When I'm sure Mr. M is in the office, I rock back and get myself balanced. My world record is three minutes and twenty-seven seconds.

★   ★   ★

I've been living in the hotel awhile now. Before that it was someplace worse, over on Fifth. Someplace where you had crackheads and hypes puking in the hallways and OD'ing in the bathrooms we shared. Someplace where you had women knocking on your door at all hours, asking could they suck your dick for five dollars. It was barely better than being on the street, which is where I ended up after my release from Lancaster. Hell, it was barely better than Lancaster.

A Mexican died in the room next to mine while I was living there. I was the one who found him, and how I figured it out was the smell. I was doing janitorial work in those days, getting home at dawn and sleeping all morning, or trying to, anyway. At first the odor was just a tickle in my nostrils, but then I started to taste something in the air that made me gag if I breathed too deeply. I didn't think anything of it because it was the middle of summer and there was no air-conditioning and half the time the showers were broken. To put it plainly, everybody stunk in that place. I went out and bought a couple of rose-scented deodorizers and set them next to my bed.

A couple of days later I was walking to my room when something strange on the floor in front of 316 caught my eye. I bent down for a closer look and one second later almost fell over trying to get up again. What it was was three fat maggots, all swole up like overcooked rice. I got back down on my hands and knees and pressed my cheek to the floor to see under the door, and more maggots wriggled on the carpet inside the room, dancing around the dead man they'd sprung from.

Nobody would tell me how the guy died, but they said it was so hot in the room during the time he lay in there that he exploded. It took a special crew in white coveralls and rebreathers almost a week to clean up the mess, and even then the smell never quite went away. It was one of the happiest days of my life when I moved from there.

J BONE'S COUSIN, the player from the lobby, is laughing at me. I'm not trying to be funny, but the man is high, so everything makes him laugh. His name is Leon.

It's 6:30 in the evening outside. In here, with tinfoil covering the windows, it might as well be midnight. I suspect time isn't the main thing on the minds of Leon and Bone and the two girls passing a blunt on the bed. They've been at it for hours already and seem to be planning on keeping the party going way past what's wise.

The door to Bone's room was wide open when I walked by after work, still wearing my uniform. I heard music playing, saw people sitting around.

"Who that, McGruff the Crime Dog?" Leon called out.

Some places it's okay to keep going when you hear something like that. Not here. Here, if you give a man an inch on you, he'll most definitely take a mile. So I went back.

"What was that?" I said, serious but smiling, not weighting it one way or the other.

"Naw, man, naw," Leon said. "I's just fucking with you. Come on in and have a beer."

All I wanted was to get home and watch *Jeopardy!*, but I couldn't say no now, now that Leon had backed down. I had to have at least one drink. One of the girls handed me a Natural Light, and Leon joked that I better not let anybody see me with it while I was in uniform.

"That's cops, man, not guards," I said, and that's what got him laughing.

"You know what, though," he says. "Most cops be getting high as motherfuckers."

Everybody nods and murmurs, "That's right, that's right."

"I mean, who got the best dope?" he continues. "Cops' girlfriends, right?"

He's wearing the same suit he had on the other day, the shirt unbuttoned and the jacket hanging on the back of his chair. He's got the gift of always looking more relaxed than any man has a right to, and that relaxes other people. And then he strikes.

"So what you guarding?" he asks me.

"A little jewelry store on Hill," I say.

"You got a gun?" he says.

"Don't need one," I say. "It's pretty quiet."

I don't tell him I'm not allowed to carry because of my record. We aren't friends yet. Some of these youngsters, first thing out of their mouths is their crimes and their times. They've got no shame at all.

"What you gonna do if some motherfucker comes in

waving a gat, wanting to take the place down?" Leon says.

I sip my beer and shrug. "Ain't my store," I say. "I'll be ducking and covering."

"Listen at him," Leon hoots. "Ducking and covering. My man be ducking and covering."

The smoke hanging in the air is starting to get to me. The music pulses in my fingertips, and my grin turns goofy. I'm looking right at the girls now, not even trying to be sly about it. The little one's titty is about to fall out of her blouse.

Leon's voice comes to me from a long way off. "I like you, man," he says. "You all right."

Satan's a sweet talker. I shake the fog from my head and down the rest of my beer. If you're a weak man, you better at least be smart enough to know when to walk away. I thank them for the drink, then hurry to my room. With the TV up loud, I can't hear the music, and pretty soon it gets back to being just like any other night.

EXCEPT THAT I dream about those girls. Dreams like I haven't dreamed in years. Wild dreams. Teenage dreams. And when I wake up humping nothing but the sheets, the disappointment almost does me in.

The darkness is a dead weight on my chest, and the hot air is like trying to breathe tar. My mind spins itself stupid, names ringing out, faces flying past. The little girl who'd lift her dress for us when we were eight or nine and show us what she got. My junior high and high-school finger bangs and fumble fucks. Monique Carter and Shawnita Weber and that one that didn't wear panties because she didn't like how they looked under her skirt. Sharon, the mother of one of my kids, and Queenie, the mother of the other. All the whores I was with when I was stationed in Germany and all the whores I've been with since.

The right woman can work miracles. I've seen beasts tamed and crooked made straight. But in order for that to happen, you have to be the right man, and I've never been anybody's idea of right.

WE CLOSE FROM one to two for lunch, and I walk over and eat a cheeseburger at the same joint every afternoon. Then I go back to the store, the old man buzzes me in, and I flip the sign on the door to Open. Today the showroom smells like Windex when I return. Mr. M's been cleaning. I sit in my chair and close my eyes. It was a slow morning—one Mexican couple, a bucktoothed kid and a pregnant girl, looking at wedding rings—and it's going to be a slow afternoon. The days fly by, but the hours drag on forever.

Around three thirty someone hits the Press for Entry button outside. The chime goes off loud as hell, goosing me to my feet. I peer through the window and see a couple of girls. I don't recognize them until the old man has already buzzed them in. It's the two from the other night, from the party in J Bone's room. They walk right past me, and if they know who I am, they don't show it.

Mr. M asks can he help them. "Let me look at this," they say, "let me look at that," and while the old man is busy inside the case, their eyes roam the store. I realize then they aren't interested in any watches or gold chains. They're scoping out the place, searching for cameras and trying to peek into the back room.

I look out the window again, and there's Leon standing on the curb with J Bone and Dallas. They've got their backs to me, but I know Leon's suit and Bone's restless shuffle. Leon throws a glance over his shoulder at the store, can't resist. There's no way he can see me through the reflections on the glass, but I duck just the same.

I go back and stand next to my chair. I cross my arms over my chest and stare up at the clock on the wall. In prison, there's a way of *being,* of making yourself invisible while still holding down your place. I feel like I'm on the yard again or in line for chow. You walk out that gate, but you're never free. What your time has taught you is a chain that hobbles you for the rest of your days.

The girls put on a show, something about being late to meet somebody. They're easing their way out.

"I could go $375 on this," the old man says, holding up a bracelet.

"We're gonna keep looking," they say.

"$350."

"Not today."

The old man sighs as they head for the door, puts the bracelet back in the case. Every lost sale stings him like it's his first. The girls walk past me, again without a glance or nod, anything that a cop studying a tape might spot. The heat rushes in when the door opens but is quickly gobbled up by the air-conditioning, and the store is even quieter than it was before the girls came in.

I don't look at Mr. M because I'm afraid he'll see how worried I am. I sit in my chair like I normally do, stare at the floor like always. The girls are right now telling Leon what they saw, how easy it would be, and J Bone is saying, *We should do it today, nigga, nobody but the old man and McGruff in there, and him with no gun.*

But Leon is smarter than that. *That ain't how we planned it,* he says. *We're gonna take our time and do it right.*

Him sending those girls in to case the store doesn't bode well for me. There's no way he didn't think I'd remember them, which means he didn't care if I did. He either figures I won't talk afterward or, more likely, that I won't be able to.

THERE ARE LOTS of Leons out there. The first one I ever met was named Malcolm, after Malcolm X. He was twelve, a year younger than me, but acted fifteen or sixteen. He was already into girls, into clothes, into making sure his hair was just right. I'd see him shooting craps with the older boys. I'd see him smoking Kools. The first time he spoke to me, I was like, *What's this slick motherfucker want with a broke-ass fool like me?* I was living in a foster home then, wearing hand-me-down hand-me-downs, and the growling of my empty stomach kept me awake at night.

Malcolm's thing was shoplifting, and he taught me how. We started out taking candy from the Korean store, the two of us together, but after a while he had me in supermarkets, boosting laundry detergent, disposable razors, and baby formula while he waited outside. Then this junkie named Maria would return the stuff to another store, saying she'd lost the receipt. We'd hit a few different places a day and split the money three ways. I never questioned why Maria and I were doing Malcolm's dirty work, I was just happy to have him as a friend. Old men called this kid sir, and the police let him be. It was like I'd lived in the dark before I met him.

The problem was, every few years after that, a new Malcolm came along, and pretty soon I'd find myself in the middle of some shit I shouldn't have been in the middle of, trying to impress him. "You know what's wrong with you?" Queenie, the mother of my son, once said. She always claimed to have me figured out. "You think you can follow someone to get somewhere, but don't nobody you know have any idea where the hell they're going either."

She was right about that. In fact, the last flashy bastard who got past my good sense talked me right into prison, two years in Lancaster. I was a thirty-three-year-old man about to get fired from Popeyes Chicken for mouthing off to my twenty-year-old boss. "That's ridiculous," Kelvin said. "You're better than that." He had a friend who ran a chop shop, he said. Dude had a shopping list of cars he'd pay for.

"Yeah, but I'm trying to stay out of trouble," I said.

"This ain't trouble," Kelvin said. "This is easy money."

I ended up going down for the second car I stole. The police lit me up before I'd driven half a block, and I never heard from Kelvin again, not a *Tough luck, bro,* nothing. It took that to teach me my lesson. I can joke about it now and say I was a slow learner, but it still hurts to think I was so stupid for so long.

·

WHEN THE HEAT breaks late in the day, people crawl out of their sweatboxes and drag themselves down to the street to get some fresh air and let the breeze cool their skin. They sit on the sidewalk with their backs to a wall or stand on busy corners and tell each other jokes while passing a bottle. The dope dealers work the crowd, signaling with winks and whistles, along with the Mexican woman who peddles T-shirts and tube socks out of a shopping cart and a kid trying to sell a phone that he swears up and down is legit.

I usually enjoy walking through the bustle, a man who's done a day of work and earned a night of rest. I like seeing the easy light of the setting sun on everybody's faces and hearing all of them laugh. Brothers call out to me and shake my hand as I pass by, and there's an old man who plays the trumpet like you've never heard anyone play the trumpet for pocket change.

I barrel past it all today, not even pausing to drop a quarter in the old man's case. My mind is knotted around one worry: what I'm gonna say to Leon. I haven't settled on anything by the time I see him and his boys standing in front of the hotel, so it won't be a pretty sermon, just the truth.

The three of them are puffing on cigars, squinting against the smoke as I roll up.

"Evening, fellas," I say.

"What up, Officer," J Bone drawls.

Dallas giggles at his foolishness, but Leon doesn't crack a smile. The boy's already got a stain on his suit, on the lapel of the coat. He blows a smoke ring and looks down his nose at me.

"I saw them girls in the store today," I say to him.

"They was doing some shopping," he says.

"I saw you all too."

"We was waiting on them."

He's been drinking. His eyes are red and yellow, and his breath stinks. I get right to my point.

"Ain't nothing in there worth losing your freedom for," I say.

"What you talking about?" Leon says.

"Come on, man, I been around," I say.

"He been around," Bone says, giggling again.

"You've got an imagination, I'll give you that," Leon says.

"I hope that's all it is," I say.

Leon steps up so he's right in my face. We're not two inches apart, and the electricity coming off him makes the hair on my arms stand up.

"Are you fucking crazy?" he says.

"Maybe so," I mumble, and turn to go. When I'm about to pull open the lobby door, he calls after me.

"How much that old man pay you?"

"He pays me what he pays me," I say.

"I was wondering, 'cause you act like you the owner."

"I'm just looking out for my own ass."

Leon smiles, trying to get back to being charming. With his kind, though, once you've seen them without their masks, it's never the same.

"And you know the best way to do that, right?" he says.

"Huh?" I say.

"Duck and cover," he says.

He's going to shoot me dead. I hear it in his voice. He's already got his mind made up.

YOUNGBLOOD SAYS HE knows someone who can get me a gun, a white boy named Paul, a gambler, a loser, one of them who's always selling something. I tell Youngblood I'll give him twenty to set it up. Youngblood calls the guy, and the guy says he has a little .25 auto he wants a hundred bucks for. That's fine, I say. I have three hundred dollars hidden in my room. It's supposed to be Mexico money, but there isn't gonna be any Mexico if Leon puts a bullet in me.

Paul wants to meet on Sixth and San Pedro at nine p.m. It's a long walk over, and Youngblood talks the whole way there about his usual nothing. He has to stop three times. Once to piss and twice to ask some shaky-looking brothers where's a dude named Breezy. I'm glad I have my money in my sock. I don't like to dawdle after dark. They'll cut you for a quarter down here, for half a can of beer.

We're a few minutes late to the corner, but this Paul acts like it was an hour. "What the fuck?" he keeps saying, "what the fuck?" looking up and down the street like he expects the police to pop out any second. He has a bandage over one eye and is wearing a T-shirt with cartoon race-horses on it, the kind they give away at the track.

"Show me what you got," I say, interrupting his complaining.

"Show you what I got?" he says. "Show me what you got."

I reach into my sock and bring out the roll of five twenties. I hand it to him, and he thumbs quickly through the bills.

"Wait here," he says.

"Hold on, now," I say.

"It's in my car," he says. "You motherfuckers may walk around with guns on you, but I don't."

He hurries off toward a beat-up Nissan parked in a loading zone.

"It's cool," Youngblood says. "Relax."

Paul opens the door of the car and gets in. He starts the engine, revs it, then drives away. I stand there with my mouth open, wondering if I misunderstood him, that he meant he was going somewhere else to get the gun and then bring it back. But that isn't what he said. Thirty years on the street, and I haven't learned a goddamn thing. I hit Youngblood so hard, his eyes roll up in his head. Then I kick him when he falls, leave him whining like a whipped puppy.

★　　★　　★

I DON'T SLEEP that night or the next, and at work I can't sit still, waiting for what's coming. Two days pass, three, four. At the hotel, I see Leon hanging around the lobby and partying in J Bone's room. We don't say anything to each other as I pass by, I don't even look at him, but our souls scrape like ships' hulls, and I shudder from stem to stern.

When Friday rolls around and still nothing has happened, I start to think I'm wrong. Maybe what I said to Leon was enough to back him off. Maybe he was never serious about robbing the store. My load feels a little lighter. For the first time in a week I can twist my head without the bones in my neck popping.

To celebrate, I take myself to Denny's for dinner. Chicken-fried steak and mashed potatoes. A big Mexican family is there celebrating something. Mom and Dad and Grandma and a bunch of kids, everyone all dressed up. I'm forty-two years old, not young anymore, but I'd still like to have something like that someday. Cancer took my daughter when she was ten, and my son's stuck in prison. If I ever make it to Mexico, maybe I'll get a second chance, and this time, this time, it'll mean something.

THEY SHOW UP at 2:15 on Saturday. We've just reopened after lunch, and I haven't even settled into my chair yet when the three of them crowd into the doorway. Dallas is in front, the hood of his sweatshirt pulled low over his face.

He's the one who pushes the buzzer, the one Leon's got doing the dirty work.

"Don't let 'em in!" I shout to Mr. M.

The old man toddles in from the back room, confused. "What?"

"Don't touch the buzzer."

Dallas rings again, then raps on the glass with his knuckles. I've been afraid for my life before—in prison, on the street, in rooms crowded with men not much more than animals—but it's not something you get used to. My legs shake like they have every other time I've been sure death is near, and my heart tries to tear itself loose and run away. I crouch, get up, then crouch again, a chicken with its head cut off.

J Bone tugs a ski mask down over his face and pushes Dallas out of the way. He charges the door, slamming into it shoulder-first, which makes a hell of a noise, but that's about it. He backs up, tries again, then lifts his foot and drives his heel into the thick, bulletproof glass a couple of times. The door doesn't budge.

"I'm calling the police!" the old man shouts at him. "I've already pressed the alarm."

Leon yells at Bone, and Bone yells at Leon, but I can't hear what they're saying. Leon also has his mask on now. He draws a gun from his pocket, and I scramble for cover behind a display case as he fires two rounds into the lock. He doesn't understand the mechanics, the bolts that shoot into steel and concrete above and below when you turn the key.

People on the street are stopping to see what's going on. Dallas runs off, followed by Bone. Leon grabs the door handle and yanks on it, then gives up too. He peels off his mask and starts to walk one way before turning quickly and jogging in the other.

I get up and go to the door to make sure they're gone for real. I should be relieved, but I'm not. I'm already worried about what's going to happen next.

"Those black bastards," Mr. M says. "Those fucking black bastards."

ONCE THEY FIND out about my record, the police get it in their heads that we were all in it together and it's just that I lost my nerve at the last minute.

How did you know not to let them in? they ask me twenty different times in twenty different ways.

"I saw the gun," I say, simple as that.

Mr. M ends up going to the hospital with chest pains, and his son shows up to square everything away. He keeps thanking me for protecting his father.

"You may have saved his life," he says, and I wish I could say that's whose life I was thinking about.

The police don't finish investigating until after six. I hang around the store until then because I'm not ready to go back to the hotel. When the cops finally pack up, I walk home slowly, expecting Leon to come out of nowhere at any minute like a lightning bolt. There'll be a gun in his hand, or a knife. He knows how it goes: if you're worried about a snitch, take him out before he talks.

I make it back safely, though. Leon's not waiting out

front or in the lobby or on the stairs. The door to J Bone's room is open, but no music is playing, and nobody's laughing. I glance in, time sticking a bit, and see that the room is empty except for a bunch of greasy burger bags and half-finished forties with cigarettes sunk in them.

I lock my door when I get inside my room, open the window, turn on the fan. My legs stop working, and I collapse on the bed, exhausted. I dig out a bottle of Ten High that I keep for when the demons come dancing and swear that if I make it through tonight, I'll treat every hour I have left as a gift.

I TALK TO the Chinaman at the desk the next morning, and he tells me J Bone checked out yesterday, ran off in a hurry. Youngblood is listening in, pretending to watch the lobby TV. We haven't spoken since I lost my temper.

"What do you know about it?" I call to him, not sure if he'll answer.

"Cost you five dollars to find out," he says.

I hand over the money, and he jumps up off the couch, eager to share. He says Leon and Bone had words yesterday afternoon, talking about the police being after them, and "You stupid," "No, you stupid." Next thing they went upstairs, came down with their shit, and split.

"Where do you think they went?" Youngblood asks me.

"Fuck if I know," I say. "Ask your friend Paul."

"He ain't my friend," Youngblood says. "I put the word out on him. I'm gonna get you your money back."

I'm so happy to have Leon gone that I don't even care about the money. I ask Youngblood if he wants to go for breakfast, my treat. He's a good kid. A couple of hours from now, after he takes his first shot, he'll be useless, but right this minute, I can see the little boy he once was in his crooked smile.

He talks about LeBron James—LeBron this, LeBron that—as we walk to McDonald's. We go back and forth from shady patches still cool as night to blocks that even this early are being scorched by the sun. Nobody's getting crazy yet, and it doesn't smell too bad except in the alleys. Almost like morning anywhere. I keep looking over my shoulder, but I can feel myself relaxing already. A couple more days, and I'll be back to normal.

MR. M'S SON told me before I left the store that it'd be closed for at least a week but not to worry because they'd pay me like I was still working. The next Thursday he calls and asks me to come down. The old man is still in the hospital, and it doesn't look like he'll be getting out anytime soon, so the son has decided to shut the store up for good. He hands me an envelope with $2,500 inside, calls it severance.

"Thank you again for taking care of my father," he says.

"Tell him I said hello and get well soon," I reply.

The next minute I'm out on the street, unemployed for the first time in years. I have to laugh. I barely gave Leon the time of day, didn't fall for his mess, didn't jump when he said to, and he still managed to fuck up the good thing I had going. That's the way it is. Every time you manage to stack a few bricks, a wave's bound to come along and knock them down.

THEY RUN GIRLS out of vans over on Towne. You pay a little more than you would for a street whore, but they're generally younger and cleaner, and doing it in the van is better than doing it behind a dumpster or in an Andy Gump. I shower and shave before I head out, get a hundred bucks from my stash behind the light switch and stick it in my sock.

Mama-san is carrying more groceries up the stairs, both kids hanging on her, as I'm going down.

"No cooking," I say. "No cooking."

She doesn't reply, but the kids look scared. I didn't mean for that to happen.

The freaks come out at night, and the farther east you go, the worse it gets. Sidewalk shitters living in cardboard boxes, ghosts who eat out of garbage cans, a blind man showing his dick on the corner. I keep my gaze forward, my hands balled into fists. Walking hard, we used to call it.

Three vans are parked at the curb tonight. I make a first pass to scope out the setup. The pimps stand together, a trio of cocky little *vatos* with gold chains and shiny shirts. My second time by, they start in hissing through their teeth and whispering, "Big tits, tight pussy."

"You looking for a party?" one of them asks me.

"What if I am?" I say.

The pimp walks me to his van and slides open the side door. I smell weed and something coconut. A chubby Mexican girl wearing a red bra and panties is lying on a mattress back there. She's pretty enough, for a whore, but I'd still like to check out what's in the other vans. I don't want to raise a ruckus though.

"How much," I say to nobody in particular.

The pimp says forty for head, a hundred for half and half. I get him down to eighty. I crawl inside the van, and he closes the door behind me. There's cardboard taped to the windshield and the other windows. The only light is what seeps in around the edges. I'm sweating already, big drops of it racing down my chest inside my shirt.

"How you doing tonight?" I say to the girl.

"Okay," she says.

She uses her hand to get me hard, then slips the rubber on with her mouth. I make her stop after just a few seconds and have her lie back on the mattress. I come as soon as I stick it in. It's been a long time.

"Can I rest here a minute?" I say.

The girl shrugs and cleans herself with a baby wipe. She has nice hair, long and black, and big brown eyes. I ask her where she's from. She says Mexico.

"I'm moving down there someday," I say.

My mouth gets away from me. I tell her I was in Germany once, when I was in the army, and that I came back and had two kids. I tell her about leaving them just like my mom and dad left me, and how you say you're never gonna do certain things, but then you do. I tell her that's why God's turned away from us and Jesus is a joke. When I run out of words, I'm crying some.

"It's okay," the girl says. "It's okay."

Her pimp bangs on the side of the van and opens the door. Time's up.

I'VE SEEN ENOUGH that I could write my own bible. For example, here's the parable of the brother who hung on and the one who fell: Two months later I'm walking home from my new job guarding a Mexican dollar store on Los Angeles. A bum steps out in front of me, shoves his dirty hand in my face, and asks for a buck. I don't like when they're pushy, and I'm about to tell him to step off, but then I realize it's Leon.

He's still wearing his suit, only now it's filthy rags. His eyes are dull and dead-looking, his lips burned black from the pipe. All his charm is gone, all his kiss-my-ass cockiness. Nobody is following this boy anymore but the reaper.

"Leon?" I say. I'm not scared of him. One punch now would turn him back to dust.

"Who you?" he asks, warily.

"You don't remember?"

He opens his eyes wide, then squints. A quiet laugh rattles his bones.

"Old McGruff," he says. "Gimme a dollar, Crime Dog."

I give him two.

"Be good to yourself," I say as I walk away.

"You're a lucky man," he calls after me.

No, I'm not, but I *am* careful. Got a couple bricks stacked, a couple bucks put away, and one eye watching for the next wave. Forever and ever, amen.

AFTER ALL

THEIR SECOND DAY OF walking, Benny said to the Bear, When we gettin' there? and the Bear said, Shit, this is nothin'. I once went a week for half a case a cream corn. Yeah, Benny said, but I told my ma only a few days, not a week. The Bear snorted. You get back with full pockets and yer ma won't be cryin' sad, he said, she'll be cryin' happy. Benny put that picture in his head and ignored the blister plaguing his toe. Good shoes were coming, and good food. He and the Bear wore masks against the dust and hoods against the sun, and they walked.

THEY WERE CHASING the Bear's dream. Back before everything, his great-great-grandpa lived in a town that was swallowed up by a government lake. The old man couldn't bring himself to leave, so when the water began to rise, he sat in the cellar of his house with a coffee can full of Krugerrands and waited to drown. What's a Krugerrand?

Benny wanted to know. A gold coin, the Bear said, and a hundred a them's a treasure. The Bear's dream was that the lake had dried up. I saw it clear, he said, and it gave me great joy, that old-time town risin' forgotten out of the water. He didn't ask the peddlers who passed by the lake or the soldiers on patrol what they'd seen for fear they'd wonder at his interest, and he only told Benny about it after swearing him in as his fifty-fifty partner. Benny could barely sleep that night, thinking of it. I mean, who besides the Bear used words like *dream* and *joy* and *treasure*? Nobody, that's who.

THEY FOLLOWED THE road but kept off the pavement. Nothing up there but trouble. The path they took through the brush had been stomped into existence by the feet of countless other cautious travelers, some of whom had carved their names into the trees: Beano and Wiseass and Clint. *Go Home Fool!* someone had written, and *Fuck All*. Benny didn't know letters, so the Bear read the words out as they passed them. The map they were using was in the Bear's memory, in case of desperadoes. Yer my boy if they ask, he said. And we heard rumor of payin' work in Kernville.

THE BEAR TALKED like he'd forgotten he was Benny's father, something Benny knew because his ma had told him, then tried to say no, not really, then said so again one night when she was drinking. Having no kin—or at least none he claimed—the Bear lived out in the scrub with the other loners. This was an old rule from right after, meant to protect the women, but it'd never worked—new bastards were born every week. Nobody was much moved to change anything, however, because everything had changed too much already. The first time Benny saw the Bear, both were in line for a free lunch some preacher was serving. The Bear gave Benny a butane lighter for his ma and half a hacksaw blade for himself. They never ever touched on the truth, understanding that it's sometimes better to let things lie. As far as it went was Benny once mouthing *Pop* behind the Bear's back and the Bear carrying Benny to the clinic after the boy broke his leg falling off a slag heap. He had to leave the room when the doc set the bone, the kid's screams too much for him.

TOWARD NIGHT THEY quit the trail and stealth-camped wherever they found cover. Dinner was FEMA grub: protein bars and vitamin cookies. They never built fires—you didn't want to announce yourself—but were warm just the same in their coats and bedrolls. Benny hadn't slept out before, and the night sounds spooked him. Swallowing his fear, he said he wished they had some music. What do you know about music? the Bear asked. Benny said, One time a show come through, a man on a guitar, another on a pinano—piano, the Bear said—piano, Benny went on, drum, horn, every damn thing. I remember some of the songs. Sing one, the Bear said. *Jesse James was a lad that killed many a man. He robbed the Danville train. And the dirty little coward that shot Mr. Howard laid poor Jesse in his grave.* The Bear clapped softly when Benny finished. Later that night, snapping twigs and rustling brush woke them both. They clutched their knives and held their breath. The moon showed a doe and two fawns high-stepping across the clearing they were camped in. Well, I'll be damned, the Bear whispered. Boo, you old ghosts, boo.

THE BEAR DID a little of everything to get by. Digging, hammering, hauling. What he mostly was, though, what he called himself, was a picker, one of those some said resourceful others said ghoulish men who ventured into blast zones to scrounge the ruins for trade goods. Pulling his cart behind him, he trekked deep into sectors that'll still be toxic a hundred years from now and came out with tools, boots, scrap metal—whatever he could get at with his shovel and pry bar. His hauls set him up pretty well—he had a small trailer to bunk in, a bicycle, a nice woodstove—but he paid for every bit of it with lost sleep. Those who ain't seen what I have can't imagine, he said, thinking of the family of skeletons he found huddled together under a bedspread, the blasphemous farewell of a priest scrawled on the wall of a church, and the newborns at the hospital shrunk to totems of leather and bone and hair. He was burdened with the final moments of towns full of corpses, bore them like a curse of constant pain.

For this reason his most closely guarded possession was a gun he'd unearthed on one of his forays and carried with him everywhere, hidden in the bottom of his ruck, a revolver so hot it set off Geigers if he wasn't careful. Just one round rested in it, the bullet the Bear called his last meal, his ticket out when the dead babies and radioactive-dust storms finally broke his spirit.

THEY WATERED UP at a spring the next day, topped off their bottles and drank their fill. A clatter coming from the road flattened them in the dirt, then drew them up the embankment on their bellies to see what was what. A squad of soldiers, regular army, was passing by, twenty or so grunts and a couple wagons drawn by bony horses. A cuffed and hooded figure sat slumped in the bed of one of the wagons, head bobbing with every pothole. I'ma ask for some food, said Benny, who'd grown up begging off soldiers in town. The Bear, with a longer memory and a scar from a rifle butt on his forehead, held him back. Keep yer mind on what yer doin', he growled. Benny scoffed at his wariness, pulled away, and scrambled out onto the pavement, where the grunts swung their guns his way and yelled for him to stop. Making no mention of the Bear, he told them the Kernville story and came away with a beef-stew MRE and a handful of Patriot hard candies, each wrapper printed with the picture and description of a wanted terrorist. The Bear wasn't where he'd left him, nor down on the trail either. Benny couldn't think of what to do but keep walking and hope to catch up to him. He didn't get a hundred yards before someone charged out of the bushes and took him hard to the ground. You go against me again, and I'll send you back to Bako, the Bear said. He wouldn't eat any of the stew and told Benny the candy was for snitches.

BENNY WAS HURT by the Bear's grousing but did with him what he did with his ma when she was down on him: He imagined him laughing. He thought of the night he hiked the hour from his house to the shantytown in the scrub, for some reason yearning to see where the Bear lived. He found him and a dozen other men circled around a bonfire, a bottle glinting as it moved from hand to hand. Their howls and scuffles and shady reputation kept Benny hidden in the bushes, but when he remembered it later, it was as if he'd been right up there with them, waving smoke, spitting into the flames, and roaring after a tug on the jug: Jesus Christ, someone call the doc, I think I been poisoned. The talk was of the old days, this geezer pining for hot water, that one going on about his dad's truck to people who'd never seen one running. Some got sad and some got bored, so it was a relief when a big bald ape called for a song. Dirty Dick sang a silly one about some Irishmen digging a ditch, then someone else told a joke about two pickers who fucked a farmer's daughter. Benny looked across the fire to see the Bear laughing like a man who'd needed to, his mouth haw-hawing and tears running down his cheeks.

Thinking about him like that now, in their cold, dark camp, made Benny smile all over again. The Bear still had some happy in him, he was sure of it.

ON THE FOURTH day, the trail dropped into a deep canyon while the road ran high above, clinging to the canyon's sheer north wall. A trickle of water snaked along the bottom of the gorge, where Benny and the Bear hopped from boulder to bone-white boulder. The Bear told Benny how it used to be a river full of fish and frogs, good eating all. Then he said, But, see, what's bad on one hand is good on the other, 'cause drought down here proves the lake up there is likely dry too, meanin' my dream now has the blessin' of science. Just before the trail began its long climb to rejoin the road, they came upon a cabin standing vacant in a grove of cottonwoods. Everything useful had been stripped from it, but the Bear nonetheless went to work with his hammer and screwdriver and in no time was stuffing twelve feet of wire, some tiny springs from a toaster, and a couple of door hinges into his pack. You know what that is? he asked Benny about a dusty, broken something lying on the floor. A TV, Benny said. What about that? the Bear asked. Computer. And that? A whatchacallit, fan, for hot days. A clearing out back held two graves, one long, one short, no marker on either. If you weren't here, I'd dig those up too, the Bear said. No, you wouldn't, Benny replied. I surely would, the Bear said. I'm just too ashamed to do it in front of you. It took the rest of the day to hike out of the canyon. Benny was glad to be close to the road again. He trusted the pavement more than he did the dirt.

THE BEAR GOT no rest that night. He told himself it was excitement about reaching the lake the next day, but he hadn't been excited about anything in years. He stared at the stars until his eyes burned, then rolled over and watched Benny sleep, envying the boy's peace. This mess, the after, was all the kid knew. Life was tough for him now and would be tough for him forever. It sometimes seemed worse, though, for old dogs like the Bear, who had memory, however faded and fading, of what it was like before. There you'd be, marching along, doing okay, when a childhood recollection of an ice-cold Popsicle on a hot summer day knocked you all the way back to mourning again. The Bear spent the rest of the night pondering how many times a man could start over and calculating the dragged dead weight of the past. He'd come to no conclusions by dawn but was cheered nonetheless by the start of the new day, the rosy reappearance of the world being a wonder that never failed to sweep away his gloom and fill his sails with enough wind to get him moving.

I ALREADY GOT my share spent, Benny said. Oh, yeah? Yeah. I made a list. They were drawing close to the bridge where they'd first catch sight of the lake and see once and for all. The cool morning had given way to a swelter, the murderous sun scorching even the air they winced into their lungs. Me and Ma can do a lot better than the old roof we got now, Benny said. Bitch is so rusted out, the rain dribbles right through. And I want a bicycle, like yours, only with chrome. There was also a dude stopped by the other week who said electricity'd be back soon and he could wire us for it. Said his rate'd be cheaper now than then, when everybody'll be after him all at once. The Bear paused in the narrow shade of a dead pine and reached under his hood to swipe the sweat off his face. Peddlers been runnin' that scam since I was a kid, he said. Ain't no electricity comin'. Benny bent for a stone, tossed it. You don't know that, he said. A grunt told me he saw lights in houses in Frisco. The Bear started walking again, couldn't stand the stupidity. If so, it was a rich man, he said over his shoulder. Richer than you no matter how many Krugerrands we find. He and Benny plodded in silence for a bit, through the heat, through the dust, thorny shrubs tugging at their pant legs. Then Benny said, You ever meet a rich man? I've *seen* a few, the Bear said, and it looked as if they died just like the poor ones. Better pickin', though. Well, Benny said, lucky for us all, the body's just a shell our souls moan through.

WHERE THE LAKE had been there was now nothing but a mudflat dried so hard it'd take a pickax to get through. Out in the middle lay the ruins of the town Benny and the Bear had come seeking, half sunk in the crust, a dun hump against the horizon in which the only signs of the hand of man were the straight lines and right angles of concrete foundations and crumbling brick walls. That it? Benny asked after he and the Bear had stared awhile from the bridge. He'd expected houses and stores, derelict cars and faded billboards. The Bear was disappointed too, but didn't show it. The water ate up most of the iron and wood, he said, but gold don't rust, so grab your gear and let's go. They walked out onto the flat, heat rippling around them. Benny raced ahead, determined to reach the town first. When he got there he slapped the wall of one of the buildings and shouted, Mine! Peering into the structure through an empty window frame, he saw more mud, clumps of dead weeds, and a few fish skeletons. Flies hovered over the mess, and the smell made his nose wrinkle. The Bear tromped among the ruins until the footprint of the town became apparent to him. He pointed out to Benny where the main drag had run and the narrower residential streets that branched off it. They found a corroded gas pump lying on its side and a couple of truck tires embedded like fossils in the dried muck.

305 Willis was the address that had been passed down in the Bear's family, the location of the house where Grandpa Pete died clutching his fortune. There were no street signs to consult, and the mailboxes had floated away. The Bear was reduced to walking around with one arm held out in front of him like a dowser's wand, counting on some ancestral polarity to lead him to his kin's remains. He gave up after an hour and started barking orders. We'll camp here. Be ready to work at first light. Stop whistlin'. They fetched

water from a creek at the edge of the flat and ate dinner in silence. Not that there was any need to talk. Benny found answers to most of his questions in the Bear's downcast eyes and muttered curses.

THE BEAR WAS already busy when Benny awoke. Kneeling next to the husk of what was once a house, he broke the dried mud that surrounded it with his screwdriver, then scraped away the dirt he made with his free hand. When he reached the foundation, he began to move along it, jabbing and digging, in search of passage into the basement. As soon as Benny approached, he tossed the kid a chisel and said, Pick yourself a house and go for it. Benny went to the next ruin and followed the Bear's lead. Stab, twist, stab, twist, scoop. Stab, twist, stab, twist, scoop. They kept to the shade, working on whatever side of the houses the sun chased it to. The Bear unearthed a faucet that still had a hose attached and called Benny over to look. A short time later, he showed him a plastic flower, part of a thing to feed birds.

Benny didn't care much about the junk. He had a blister on his finger, and his back hurt from bending. His progress slowed after a while, and finally whenever he knew the Bear couldn't see him, he quit digging completely and sat against the wall and stared out at the mountains rising hazed in the distance. The Bear was flagging too, until his screwdriver hit something that made a hollow sound. In a few frenzied minutes he'd scraped away enough dirt to reveal the remains of a wooden door. Hey, he called, hey!, eager for Benny to know they weren't wasting their time. The kid came running, and they yanked at the rotten boards until they gave way, but all they got for the effort was more mud. The basement was full of it, up to the ceiling.

The Bear had built up so much momentum by now, he couldn't stop. He and Benny worked together, him breaking ground, and the kid carrying off the muck. After an hour of this they'd exposed only the first two steps of the stairs leading down. Benny took a break, went up and sprawled on what had been the porch of the house. An object half buried in the mud got his attention, its color a brilliant blue that flashed against the infinite drab surrounding it. He wiggled the thing free and dragged it back to show the Bear, who, even after he pawed the sweat from his eyes, didn't see the meaning of the mangled sheet of siding until Benny pointed out the numbers painted on it: 412. You got the wrong place, Benny said.

THE BEAR BUGGED then, started punching the mud and screaming, Fuck! Fuck! Fuck! He kicked the siding out of Benny's hand and stomped off to another house on another street and knelt to dig there in the full sun, stabbing wildly at the earth. Benny returned to the porch and watched him give up on that ruin and move to another, then another. The wind rushed in, and with it the dust, which stung like bees when it hit bare skin. Benny took cover in the crevice he and the Bear had excavated. He hunkered down with their bedrolls and rucks and struggled to keep them from blowing away. A moaning filled the air, violent gusts shook the vestiges of the town, and the light of day was choked down to almost nothing.

The Bear welcomed the storm. It gave him something to do battle with. He was half crazy and knew it, digging here, digging there, first with a gambler's determination to turn his luck, and then, finally, merely in defiance of the blow. He swallowed mud; he made his hands bloody claws; he flew from ruin to ruin, stabbing, scraping, and growling. And when the wind ceased and the dust settled, he collapsed in such a broken posture that Benny worried he'd died. He lay where he'd fallen until the first stars showed themselves. Benny ignored him when he finally limped into camp, sat with his back to him and sucked on the last of the soldiers' candy. You didn't know how it'd be, the kid said without turning around. Ain't no shame in that. The Bear stretched out on his blanket and fell asleep tonguing the dirt and sweat off his lips and counting a coyote's yips. Benny sat up in the busy dark, pretending he was alone, testing how it felt. It was nothing he'd choose, he concluded, but something he could tolerate.

THEY BOTH WOKE raw and peevish, as if their dreams—the Bear's of the past, Benny's of the future—had butted heads all night, warring to a stalemate that left the dreamers stranded in the dreary present with neither nostalgia nor expectation as a balm. After a polite breakfast, the Bear gathered his tools and made ready to go to work. Benny rose to follow, the muscles in his back and legs groaning, but the Bear waved him off. You take it easy, he said, and walked by himself to the town's main street, where he ducked into the first structure he came to and began to probe the dried mud that covered the floor and to chisel at the walls. Benny got bored sitting by himself, got hot, and eventually scuffed over to join him. He found the Bear pulling wire out of a hole in the ceiling. The Bear showed him how to coil it by laying it across his palm then wrapping it around his elbow again and again.

They went from ruin to ruin in search of salvage that had survived the flood. Benny had no eye for it, so he waited for the Bear to point him to a spot. If it was a wall, the moldy plaster gave way to reveal a length of pipe. If it was the floor, there, hidden under six inches of dirt, was a stack of plastic funnels or some lead sinkers. It was as if yesterday had never happened. The Bear had his magic back. They scrounged the gas station, the grocery store, and the little Baptist church, then started on the houses. The heat was against them again but didn't seem so awful today, with all the booty they were piling up. Still, Benny worked himself dizzy and had to lie in the shade for a while. He woke from a surprise nap, and the sun was sinking fast. The Bear was crouched in the street, sorting the haul and stuffing the best of it into Benny's ruck. Go on and gather some wood, he said. We'll have a fire tonight. Is it safe? Benny asked. You don't trust me? the Bear said with a laugh, then tossed Benny two cans of chili he'd hauled all the way up from

Bako. They were supposed to be the celebration when they found the Krugerrands, but they'd squeezed enough something out of nothing today to have earned a feast.

THE BEAR CHUCKED more wood onto the fire, and what was already burning snapped and sparked and spit. He'd just told Benny he wasn't going back with him the next morning, and tending to the blaze was his way of avoiding any discussion. But the kid wouldn't be bullied. Why? he asked. What's wrong? The Bear opened his shirt for an answer, had Benny feel the lumps under his arms and on his neck. Picker cancer, he said. It came on quick and's been getting worse. You ain't seen it kill a man, but I have, and I won't do that kind of suffering. Benny was stripped of words. He sat there and toed the dust, shaken by new vistas of sorrow. I'd hoped to leave you and yer ma something, the Bear continued. The gold's a bust, but what's in that ruck'll trade for a new roof. You can have my bike too, and the trailer and everything in it. And yer gun, Benny said, hand that over too. Ha! the Bear said, lifting the pistol out of his pocket just enough that Benny could see it. I appreciate the sentiment, but I got my mind made up.

The flames leaped for an instant and caught the two of them staring into each other's eyes, but then the flickering darkness returned, and Benny was alone on his side of the fire, trying to reconstruct his world without the Bear in it, while the Bear on his side batted away a few regrets. I don't know what to do, Benny wailed. It's simple, the Bear said.

You follow the road back to Bako. You get a job in town, something regular, no picking. You meet a girl, get married, have kids. You get a house. You get electricity. You hope. Simple. Benny fell asleep eventually, wrapped in his blankets by the fire. The Bear smiled, remembering what it was like to be that kind of tired and to wake in the morning a clean slate. The flames died, and the last of the wood burned down to pulsing embers. The Bear saw castles in them, jewels, and dancing women. At dawn's first pinking he struck out across the lake bed for the high mountains to the east. A day or two and he'd find what he was looking for, a prettier place to put an end to it.

ON HIS WAY back, Benny stopped at the cabin at the bottom of the canyon. The graves were shallow, and it didn't take him long to dig them out. He found nothing in either but bones, bones he dodged in his dreams that night, bones that clicked and clacked and kept coming for him. The second day he got it into his head that he was being tested, the Bear spying on him from the bushes to see how he did on his own. Show yourself, he shouted when he could no longer stand the feeling of being watched, but not a leaf stirred and no silver-bearded mug appeared. Benny walked on, whistling away his disappointment with two Irishmen, two Irishmen and Jesse James and savoring a vision of a hot meal, a soft bed, and a once-dark room livid with incandescent light.

SWEET NOTHING

Troy pokes his head out of the bedroom as soon as I come in from work. He's got that look, like he's been up all night and made an important decision. I've seen it before. When he was going to study hypnosis and open a clinic. When he was going to move to Berlin to marry some girl he met online. When he thought he had the lottery figured out.

"Want to go for a walk?" he says.

Troy weighs 450 pounds. He has no chin, no waist, hasn't seen his dick in years except in a mirror. The only time he leaves the apartment is once a week to drive to the supermarket, and then it takes him fifteen minutes to haul himself back up the stairs from the carport to our place after paying a kid from the neighborhood to carry his bags.

And he wants to go for a walk?

"Around the block," he says. "For exercise."

I'm beat. Still can't get used to working nights. It's the kind of constant fatigue where you feel like you're floating an inch off the ground, where you see things out of the corner of your eye that aren't really there. Right now all I want is to guzzle a few beers and hit the hay, but Troy is my only friend in the world, and that should mean something.

So: "Sure," I say. "Let's go for a walk."

First come the stairs. Troy clutches the rail with both hands and descends sideways. Two steps, rest. Two steps, rest. I cradle his elbow in my palm.

We're on the second floor of one of those open-air complexes that's wrapped around a few messy beds of tropical greenery and a tiny swimming pool. The sun only shines on the water for an hour or so in the middle of the day, when it's directly overhead. This early, the pool is still in shadow. The deck chairs are empty, and a beer can drifts aimlessly in the deep end.

"You're doing great," I say to Troy when he reaches the bottom of the stairs.

He's better on level ground, more sure of himself. We walk past the mailboxes to the gate and push out of the complex into the bright, blaring morning. Gardeners are doing their thing all up and down the street, lawn mowers and leaf blowers, and a disgruntled garbage truck snatches up dumpsters, flips them over to empty them, then slams them back to the pavement.

It was hot yesterday, and it's supposed to be hotter today. Troy wipes the sweat off his forehead with the back of his hand. He hikes up his pajama bottoms and sets off stiff-legged down the sidewalk toward Hollywood Boulevard, his arms extended out from his sides to help him balance.

"Damn, man," I say. "You sprinkle speed on your Wheaties?"

"I've got to start taking care of myself," he huffs. "If I don't do something about my weight, I'll be dead in five years. And I don't want to die."

"Me neither," I say, "I don't want to die either," but that's a lie. Sometimes I do.

Troy only makes it as far as the liquor store before running out of steam. A hundred yards. He leans against the building and gulps air like a flopping fish. His face is bright red, and his Lakers jersey is soaked with perspiration. I ask if he's okay.

"Will you go in and get me a Coke?" he says, fishing in his pocket for a dollar. "Diet."

I bring the soda out to him. He drains it quickly, and we start back to the apartment.

"Tomorrow I'll go a little farther," he says. "And the day after that, even farther."

I'm pulling for the man, definitely, but I remember the hypnosis clinic, Berlin, and the lottery, so the best I can do for now is humor him.

A lemon drops off a tree and rolls across the sidewalk. I nearly trip and fall trying to get out of the way. Time for bed.

I NEVER THOUGHT about life before mine started to go wrong. I just lived it, like everybody else. But then you lose your job, and your wife leaves you for the neighbor and takes your kids, and you go from whiskey to weed to coke to crack just like the commercials warn you will. You lie and cheat and steal until one night you find yourself holding a knife on this guy, Memo, who's supposed to be your buddy, your partner in crime, and Memo gets the jump on you and gives you a concussion and you come to in jail the next day, bleeding out of your ear.

Stuff like that raises questions: Why me? What next? Where will it end?

THE SUBWAY I work at is half a block from a hospital, which is where most of our customers come from. The restaurant is open twenty-four hours, and I'm on from midnight to nine a.m. Some nights are dead, just me and the radio, and other nights it's so crazy that I'm tempted to tear off my apron and call it quits. The reason I don't is that this is what starting over is like. It's hard. It's minimum wage and night shifts and managers who are fifteen years younger than you.

I got this job after rehab, when I transitioned into a sober-living facility, and I'm still here, ten months later. The part of me that once made a hundred thousand a year and had four salesmen under him is unimpressed, but the part of me that was living in a park and breaking into vending machines for dope money can't thank me enough.

Two Korean teenagers slink into the restaurant around 2:30 a.m. One of them is holding a bloody T-shirt to his shoulder. He slumps, pale and silent, in a booth while his friend orders sandwiches.

"Your buddy all right?" I ask.

"He got shot," the kid at the counter replies. "We're going to Kaiser after."

People do this a lot, stop in on their way to the emergency room. They eat something first because they know they'll have to wait hours to be seen. A guy came in a couple weeks ago with a nail through his foot. He'd been messing around drunk with a friend's tools. Said it didn't hurt except where the nail was touching bone.

I check the booth after the kids leave, wipe away a smear of blood. My favorite show is on the radio, *After Midnight*. The host is talking to a man who found a hole in the ground that he claims is a portal into hell. He lowered a microphone into it and recorded the screams of the tortured souls.

"That's ancient Latin," the man who discovered the hole says.

"What are they saying?" the host asks.

" 'Save me.' "

About four a woman comes in and orders a cup of coffee. It's rare I get a lone female at this hour, and when I do, she's usually bundled up like an Eskimo and pushing a shopping cart. This chick is gorgeous. Arab. Armenian, maybe. Tall and thin with olive skin and long black hair. She's wearing jeans and a pink blouse, a white sweater over that.

"You work at the hospital?" I ask as I slide her cup across the counter.

"No," she says with some kind of accent. "My daughter is there."

I notice that her eyes are red and swollen and that her mascara is smeared, and I feel bad. Here she is, going through some sort of tragedy, and I was imagining what she'd look like naked.

"No charge," I say, waving away her money.

"Please," she says. "Take it."

"Really. My treat."

She pushes the bills into the tip jar. Her fingernails have been chewed to the quick. She sits in the booth by the window and stares out at the electric orange night. A bus blows past full of people going to work, and I begin to prep for the morning rush. After an hour, the woman tosses her cup in the trash and calls out a thank-you as she leaves. The pale creep of dawn is filling in the blanks outside. Another goddamn Tuesday, gentlemen. Let's make this one mean something.

I WALK WITH Troy again when I get home. He goes twice as far, almost to where Spaghetti Factory used to be, where they're putting in more condos.

"I think I'm losing weight already," he says.

I check my e-mail on his computer while he's in the shower. There's something from my son, who'll be four-teen in September. *Sick Shit* is the subject. It's a video of a kickboxer getting his leg broken in the ring, his knee snap-ping back the wrong way. I almost puke watching it. Every month or so the boy sends me something like this. Never a message, just a clip from YouTube, usually disturbing.

I haven't seen him or his little sister in three years. My ex and the neighbor packed them off to Salt Lake City after they were married, and there was nothing this here crackhead could do about it. I was actually kind of happy they left. The kids were getting to an age where they'd notice my shaking hands during our once-a-month lunches at Pizza Hut, my red eyes, the smell of booze on my breath.

The last straw was when Gwennie, my daughter, found a bloody syringe in the glove compartment of the car I'd borrowed to drive down to Orange County for our visit. The rig wasn't mine, but I still had to do some fast talking about how diabetic kitties need shots just like people do. That story always got a laugh from some asshole when I shared it at meetings.

I don't go to AA anymore, and right now I'm so glad. I grab a can of Bud out of the refrigerator. I'll never touch drugs again, but I need my three after-work beers. They're all I have to look forward to these days.

Troy's got *Kelly's Heroes* and asks if I want to watch it with him. Maybe it'll take my mind off my kids. He has a fifty-five-inch TV in his room, surround sound. I sit on the floor with my back against his bed. When the movie's over, he says he's going to order some chicken, but I'm not hungry. I'm not tired either, so I go down to the pool.

It's nice. A breeze is blowing through the courtyard, and birds chatter in the bamboo and banana trees that fill the lava-rock planters. The pool mirrors the square of blue sky above it, clouds floating in the water. I take a deep breath all the way from my gut and pop open my last beer of the day.

The new people spill out of their ground-floor unit with towels and sunscreen and a pitcher of something. A guy and a girl, early twenties. They moved in a couple weeks ago and have already thrown two parties the property manager had to shut down. The guy's playing music on his phone, the kind of shit kids dance to these days.

"This gonna bother you?" he asks, pointing at the phone.

"Not me," I say.

They're both tall and tan and in great shape. She has blond hair and big fake boobs; he's darker, with a tattoo of a thorny rose wrapped around one thick bicep. They look like advertisements for something you want and want and then realize you didn't really need.

A police helicopter flies low over the complex. The girl whoops and lifts her bikini top to flash it. When she sees me watching, she yanks the top down and says, "Oops. Sorry."

The guy waves the blue plastic pitcher and calls out, "Margarita?"

I show him my beer. "Thanks anyway."

I can tell he's going to sit next to me as soon as he offers the drink. He's got a buzz on and wants to talk to someone who won't know when he's lying and might get some of his jokes. His girlfriend is hot, he'll say, *but just between you and me, bro, dumb as a bag of rocks.*

He's Edward, she's Star.

"Star?" I say. "Really?"

"Her parents had high hopes," Edward explains.

The two of them are in from Miami to test the waters. If

something happens and they decide to stay, the first thing they'll do is get out of this shit hole and buy a house in the Hills with the money Edward is due from some kind of settlement. He's been bartending to keep busy, and Star dances at a nightclub. I give them six months out here, tops.

"What do you do?" Edward wants to know before he's even asked my name.

Star is on the other side of the pool, where the sun is brightest, on her stomach on a chaise.

"I was a sales director," I say. "Industrial refrigeration units."

"If you hear of anything in entertainment, I'm available," Edward says.

The guy's not even listening to me. That's okay. I sip my beer and stare at his girlfriend's ass. I haven't had sex since sober-living, when this Oxy fiend and I snuck off to the laundry room.

"You live with that fat guy," Edward says.

"Troy," I reply.

"That's got to be weird. Does he stink?"

I had the same sort of questions in the beginning. I found Troy on Craigslist when I was looking for a place. His last roommate had skipped out suddenly, and he needed someone to make rent for the month. It was six hundred dollars for the bedroom or three hundred for the futon in the living room. I took the futon.

I'd never lived with a fat man before and wondered how it would be. He eats a lot, of course. Large pizzas, quarts of ice cream, a box of doughnuts in fifteen minutes flat. He sleeps in a sitting position, propped up on the bed with pillows, something to do with his breathing. And he snores, man. He snores like a car that's ready to conk out. That's the only good thing about working nights.

He wasn't always so big. He showed me photos of himself when he was in high school, and he looked like a jock back then. He got sad, though. He came out here from Ohio to be an actor but ended up office manager for a chiropractor, and that did him in, the disappointment, after being so sure he was born to do something special. He let himself go, lost his job, and now he squeaks by on disability and the occasional check from his parents.

"Does he lay like the biggest shits you've ever seen?" Edward continues.

"Troy's great," I say.

Edward is already on to something else, the time Sean Penn showed up at the bar where he works. I let him finish the story, then go upstairs. I can tell I won't be able to get to sleep, that I'm going to lie on the futon and listen to the afternoon pass on the other side of the blinds while thinking about my kids and how I've probably fucked them up for life and wishing it was like it used to be, when I could knock myself senseless with whatever was at hand.

A COUPLE OF days later the Arab woman shows up at the restaurant again, at four a.m., just like last time. There are dark circles under her green eyes, and her fingers tremble when she passes me the money for her coffee.

"How's your daughter?" I ask.

Her response gets caught in her throat. She swallows hard, and a tiny, perfect tear slides down her cheek.

"Aww, hey, I'm sorry," I say.

I duck under the counter and pop up beside her, but then I'm at a loss, not sure what I was planning to do. I can't just stand there, so I pick up her coffee and guide her to a booth.

"Thank you," she says as she sinks into the seat.

I hustle back to the counter and grab some napkins. She takes one and dabs her eyes with it.

"Sit," she says, "please," so I do. There's a long silence while she pulls herself together. I look down at my knuckles, up at the buzzing fluorescent light on the ceiling. It's uncomfortable being so close to someone else's pain.

"My name is Zalika," she finally says.

"Dennis," I reply. "Nice to meet you."

"Thank you for asking about my daughter."

I was flirting when I did, trying to show that I remembered her, hoping for a smile.

"Unfortunately, she's not doing well," Zalika continues. "She was hit by a car and hurt very badly. She's been in a coma for a week now."

They were jaywalking across Vermont, Zalika and her twelve-year-old daughter, Amisi. Zalika made it to the curb first and reached into her purse for her ringing phone. A car came barreling out of the setting sun, out of nowhere. The driver slammed on his brakes, but it was too late. Zalika heard the first thud, as the car hit Amisi and sent her

194

flying through the air, and the second, when Amisi crashed back to earth.

She turned and called for her daughter, her heart refusing to acknowledge what her brain already knew. Amisi! Where had she gotten to? That couldn't be her, that tiny thing lying twisted and bloody in the gutter, arms and legs all at strange angles. Amisi!

"Don't touch her," someone yelled.

Two strong men held Zalika back, and she wanted to kill them. A woman tried to soothe her, knelt in front of her and spoke to her like a child. Zalika spit in her face.

Amisi has been in the hospital ever since, tethered to our world by tubes that feed her, fill her lungs with air, and filter the poison from her blood. Zalika is at her bedside constantly, except for when she steps out for these early-morning coffee breaks.

"The doctors don't say it's hopeless, but I can hear it in their voices," Zalika says. "They're giving me time to say good-bye, but soon they'll lose patience."

She raises her cup to her lips and takes a drink to stop herself from talking, as if by not voicing the future, she can escape it. And what can I do but say what everyone says in a moment like this? "Don't give up hope. Anything can happen."

Zalika doesn't smile, but something softens in her expression.

"You don't really believe that, do you?" she says.

"No," I reply.

"Good."

The door buzzes, and two Filipino girls in pink scrubs enter. I return to the counter to help them. Zalika leaves while I'm filling their order.

TROY SHOWS ME a bag of lettuce.

"Should I get an extra for you?" he asks.

I came to the supermarket with him because I didn't have anything better to do.

"Sure," I say. "I'll grab some dressing."

All Troy eats now is soup, salad, and Cheerios. A diet he found online. I mostly live off sandwiches from work, one at the beginning of my shift and one at the end.

"You need to watch what you put in your body too," Troy says as he pushes the cart toward the tomatoes. "Just because you're not a fat pig like me doesn't mean you're not fucking yourself up. You've got to plan your meals."

"I'm more of a one-day-at-a-time guy," I say.

"Come on, man," Troy scoffs. "Don't let that AA bullshit bleed over into your real life. You know what's wrong with most drunks? They're all *about* taking it one day at a time. They don't think ahead. If they did, they'd say, 'I'm not gonna get loaded tonight because I have to go to work tomorrow.' It's not one day at a time, it's a hundred days at a time. You have to take control of your life."

Troy is one of those people who get on track for a week and suddenly have the answers for everybody. I'll remember to ask him about his amazing self-control when he's back to making a meal out of a bag of chocolate chip cookies.

And I do have a plan. Step one: Save money. That's why I eat at work. That's why I sleep on a futon. I've got about a grand squirreled away already. Step two: Get a better job. My applications are in at Best Buy and Fry's. I'm ready to jump back into it. Put me on the floor and watch me go. Step three: See my kids, show them I'm doing better.

Troy drops some tomatoes into the cart, and we roll over to the soup aisle. He needs ten cans of chicken noodle, ten cans of vegetable beef. My head hurts when I tap my temple. I stand there tapping, hurting myself, while Troy counts out his Campbell's.

On his way to the checkstand he brushes against a spaghetti-sauce display. The thing topples over, jars exploding wetly when they hit the floor, sauce splashing everywhere. Troy is mortified. His face flushes bright red as a kid in an apron rushes over.

"Are you okay, sir?" the kid asks.

"I'm fine," Troy says. His pajama bottoms are spattered with sauce.

I tell the kid that was a dumb spot to stack breakables, right in the aisle. What if it had been a toddler who knocked them over? I know he has no say in where the displays go, but I'm doing it for Troy, so everybody doesn't assume the accident happened because he's fat.

Troy's quiet in the car on the way back to the apartment. I notice he's limping as we climb the stairs. I'm drinking beer and reading Stephen King when he calls me into the bathroom, where he's sitting on the toilet in his underwear.

A shard of glass is sticking out of his massive calf above a trickle of blood. It's a piece of one of the jars.

"Pull this out for me," he says.

I kneel beside him and grip the glass with my thumb and forefinger. A quick yank is all it takes. More blood starts to flow. Troy doesn't want to see a doctor. He asks me to patch him up as best I can. I rinse the cut, spread Neosporin on it, and wrap his leg in gauze.

A few minutes later he comes into the living room and asks if I want to go for a walk.

"Maybe you should skip today," I say.

"Nah, dude, I'm good," he says. "Let's do it."

I'm suddenly tired as hell, like I've taken a pill.

"I'm burnt," I say. "Sorry."

I lie on the futon, and I'm dreaming before Troy makes it down the stairs.

WHAT WENT WRONG? That's another question I ask myself.

My parents? They were distant but kind. Both worked at the same insurance company, and when they asked my sister and me how we were doing each evening at dinner, the answer they wanted and got was "Fine." We held up our end of the bargain; they held up theirs. A little bloodless, but better than the messes I've made.

My wife? Okay, we married too young and hung on too long. We were casually cruel to each other, and torment became a game for us. But that's nothing unusual. You see it on TV every day. I can't blame the kids either, although when they came along I had to divide what love I had in me into smaller portions, and it sounds selfish, but you know who got shorted? Me.

As for work, I've only met two people, a dope dealer and a marine, who truly enjoyed what they did for a living and wouldn't walk away from it if they had the opportunity. A job is what you do to pay the bills. Some are better than others, but they're all painful in a way. It's a pain you learn to live with, however, not the kind that breaks you.

So what, then, spun me out, sent me sliding across the track and into the wall? Maybe I'm not meant to know. Maybe if all of us were suddenly able to peer into our hearts and see all the wildness there, the wanting, the fire and black smoke, we'd forget how to fake it, and the whole rotten world would jerk to a halt. There's something to be said for the truth, sure, but the truth is, it's lies that keep us going.

I STOP AT Goodwill to buy a sport coat and tie on my way to my interview. They cost me fifteen dollars. Best Buy called yesterday and said to come in at one and ask for Harry. The store is on Santa Monica and La Brea, so if I get the job, I can take the same bus I do now.

The chick at the customer-service desk has blond hair and black eyebrows. She's a big girl, and her clothes are too tight. She looks me over with a smirk when I say I'm there to see Harry, wondering why a man my age would want a college student's job.

Harry's just a kid too, but he's already going bald. His handshake is an embarrassment. I will eat him alive.

He leads me through the store toward his office. A hip-hop song is booming out of the car-stereo department as we pass by. Every other word is *motherfucker*. Two employees in blue polos are staring at the speakers mounted on the wall and bobbing their heads in time to the music.

"Hey!" Harry yells at them, his voice a frustrated squeak. "What did I tell you guys?"

"Sorry, man," one of the employees says while reaching out to lower the volume. We move on, and I turn back to see the guy and his buddy bumping fists and laughing up their sleeves.

Harry's office is a windowless box off the stockroom, barely big enough for a desk and two chairs. We sit so close together, I can see the sweat beading on his greasy forehead.

"So, uh"—he picks up my application and looks down at my name—"Dennis," he says. "Why do you want to work at Best Buy?" He barely listens as I give my spiel about how my divorce threw me for a loop, but now I'm back on my feet and eager to use my sales experience at a leading chain like this one.

When I say, "Put me out on that floor, and I don't care if it's batteries, I'll be the best battery salesman you ever had," Harry just nods and starts telling me about benefits. I notice that his hands are shaking and he's breathing funny. The guy is falling apart, and I'm pretty sure I know why.

When we get to the part where he asks, "Do you have

any questions for me?" I say, "How long have you been manager?"

Harry fiddles with the name tag on his vest, the one that reads *Harry Sarkissian, Manager*. "Almost two months," he says.

"It gets easier," I say. "I know. I used to be a manager myself."

Harry's eyes fill with tears. "I bought a book from Amazon," he says. "*First, Break All the Rules*. But it's like for offices and stuff, not stores."

"You want a tip?" I say. "Something that worked for me?"

"Okay," Harry says.

"Blame everything on your bosses, the people higher up than you. Those guys out there, that music. Tell them the district manager got a complaint and said you had to do something about it. Act like you couldn't care less, but the boss is on your ass, so you've got to get on theirs. Everyone understands shit rolls downhill. They can't be mad at you, because you're just following orders."

"That might work," Harry says.

"I guarantee it will," I say. "You want another tip?"

"Sure."

"Hire me. You won't be sorry."

I laugh to let him know he can take that as a joke, and he laughs too. We shake hands again, and he walks me to the front of the store and says he'll call when he makes his decision, either way.

I'm feeling fine for once, even though it's hot out on the

street and the smog leaves a chemical taste on my tongue. I pulled what could have been a disastrous interview out of the fire and did my good deed for the day all at the same time. Baby steps toward something better.

I buy a fruit cup from a pushcart parked on the sidewalk in front of the store. The kid selling them sprinkles chili powder over the chunks of pineapple, melon, and mango, and I eat it sitting on a cinder-block wall in the thin strip of shade cast by a palm tree. My bus arrives just as I reach the stop. If I believed in luck, I might think mine had turned.

THE ONE-EYED COWBOY lingers at the counter after paying for his coffee and jabbers on and on about how he got bitten by a Great Dane when he was eight years old. I pull on plastic gloves and go back to refilling the ham and turkey bins, but he doesn't get the hint.

"To this day I get the shakes around a big dog," he says. "With little ones, I won't pet 'em, but they don't scare me."

"Huh," I say. I cut open a bag of Swiss cheese slices. "Wow."

The guy's wearing a black cowboy hat, scuffed snakeskin boots, and a bolo tie with a silver scorpion slide. His empty eye socket is a raw, red hole that made my stomach flip when I first saw it. What he's doing on Sunset Boulevard at three in the morning, I couldn't tell you.

"Now this"—he reaches up to tug the eyelid hanging loosely over the hole—"happened in a fight in Kansas City. Motherfucker got me with a broken bottle."

He's still telling stories fifteen minutes later as the door swings shut behind him and he swaggers off down the sidewalk. I wonder what it's like when the dam finally breaks and everything comes spilling out. Maybe you feel better or maybe you drown.

They're talking about UFOs on *After Midnight*. Are we being watched? Zalika shows up at four. It's been a week since I last saw her, and I'm more excited than I should be. My plan is to tell her something about my life in order to break the ice between us, about Troy wanting to lose weight and me trying to help him. The look on her face stops me cold, though. She barely glances at me when she orders her coffee and keeps dabbing at her nose with a Kleenex.

"Rough night?" I say.

She nods, tears glittering in her beautiful eyes. I want to reach out and smooth away the worry lines on her forehead, the creases at the corners of her mouth. Instead, I watch her walk alone to the booth in front of the window, where she slumps over her coffee.

"What could these extraterrestrials possibly want from us?" the host of *After Midnight* asks the expert. "We're like insects compared to them."

I continue with the breakfast prep until Zalika suddenly wails and clutches her chest.

"What's wrong?" I say as I hurry over and crouch beside her.

"They're taking Amisi off the ventilator tomorrow," she says.

We're in each other's arms then, just like that, just like when you reach out to stop someone from falling. She sobs on my shoulder, and I rub her back gently while murmuring, "I'm sorry," again and again.

When she calms down, we sit across from each other in the booth. I hand her a napkin, and she wipes her eyes and fixes her hair.

"I'm ashamed for you to see me like this," she says.

"I'm ashamed for you to see me like *this*," I reply. "Is there anyone at the hospital with you? Your husband?"

Anger slides across her face like a cloud shadow passing over the desert.

"We divorced three years ago," she says. "He took our son and moved back to Egypt. I chose to remain here, hoping it would be better for Amisi."

"A friend, then? Do you want me to call someone?"

"Thank you, but no. That's not my way."

I understand. We don't ask for help, people like us. We do our suffering in private, do our grieving in the dark.

"Let me get you more coffee," I say. I go behind the counter and refill her cup, but she's up and ready to leave by the time I return to the booth.

"I'm going," she says.

To watch her daughter slip away. To say good-bye.

"Stay strong," I say.

She turns and waves, and the morning of another terrible day creeps up on us like a thug with a lead pipe.

★　　★　　★

"CHECK ME OUT," Troy says.

He stands in the doorway to the bedroom wearing a pair of jeans that's as big as three pairs of mine. He pulls on the waistband until there's a gap of about two inches between his stomach and the pants.

"I couldn't even fit in these a month ago."

I can see it in his face too. The walking and the dieting are paying off. He's definitely slimming down.

He wants to celebrate by going to a movie. I'm not in the mood, but he hasn't been to a theater in years, and I can't say no after he offers to pay my way.

There's almost nobody in the audience at noon on a Wednesday. A gang of fidgety kids on summer vacation and the harried mommy overseeing them. A worn-out old man toting a collection of battered shopping bags who's just paying for a comfortable seat and air-conditioning, a couple hours off the street.

The armrests lift up, so Troy has plenty of room. He's excited, telling me all about the movie before the lights go down. He's been looking forward to it for months. I don't know why. It's a horror film, vampires fighting werewolves. Dumb. One of the actresses looks a lot like Zalika. She's supposed to be evil, but I root for her anyway. Of course, she dies in the end.

We stroll down Hollywood Boulevard afterward, check out the stars on the sidewalk, the handprints. Some asshole dressed like Charlie Chaplin follows Troy, imitating his lumbering gait while the tourists laugh. I want to punch him in the mouth.

★   ★   ★

EDWARD OFFERS ME a cigar, but I turn him down. It's two p.m., and most of the pool is in shade. Star is floating in the last sunny patch on a blow-up raft, wailing along to a song only she can hear through her headphones.

Edward is pissed. His car got towed last night, and he doesn't have the money to bail it out. He asks if I'll loan him three hundred dollars. I tell him I'm broke.

"What about Fatty?" he says.

Things haven't been going well for Edward. He was laid off from his job, his new tattoo got infected, and now the car. The dude is furious, all jacked up on resentment and indignation. His bare foot taps out a spastic beat on the cement of the pool deck, and he keeps tightening and releasing the muscles in his neck and jaw.

A jet slides across the blue rectangle of open sky above us. I finish my beer and wonder if I'll be able to sleep today. Star pulls herself onto the lip of the pool. She throws back her head and shakes out her hair like there's a camera on her. Edward exhales a cloud of stinking smoke. He points at Star with the red-hot cherry of his stogie and asks me, "How much do you think someone would pay to fuck that?"

MONDAY AT EIGHT a.m. I'm making breakfast sandwiches for a couple of cops and trying to figure out what to do on my night off. The big cop is teasing the little cop about something, and the little cop doesn't want to hear it. He keeps turning away and saying, "Okay, man, okay." They both have shaved heads and perfect white teeth.

Zalika walks into the restaurant, and I almost don't recognize her. That I've never seen her in the daytime might be part of it, but she's also carrying herself differently, back straight, head held high. She has a big smile on her face, and suddenly I'm smiling too. The cops look over their shoulders to see what could make a man light up that way.

She steps to the counter when they rush off to respond to a call. She reaches out to take my hand, and a thousand volts of something leap from her into me and sizzle up my arm into my chest.

"You won't believe it," she says.

"What?"

"Amisi came out of the coma an hour before they were supposed to disconnect her, and she's breathing on her own now."

I'm as excited as if it were one of my own kids. I let out a whoop and slap the counter.

"The doctors are amazed," Zalika continues. "There seems to be no permanent damage."

A few nurses walk up and stand behind Zalika, waiting to order.

"You want coffee?" I ask her.

"No, no, I've had too much already." She moves aside and motions the nurses forward. "Please, go ahead."

I make the nurses' sandwiches, wrap them, bag them. Zalika waits patiently.

"So what happens next?" I ask when the nurses leave.

"She's being transferred to a hospital in Glendale," Zalika says. "It's closer to home and has an excellent rehabilitation program. She'll be in physical therapy for a month or so but should be able to start school with her friends in September."

And then it hits me: she's here to say good-bye. I keep smiling, but my mind races behind it. I picture the two of us sitting down to dinner in a quiet restaurant, me in my Goodwill jacket and tie. She leans across the table and says, "Tell me about yourself," and where do I start? "Well, I once had to explain a bloody syringe to my nine-year-old."

More customers pile in. A cabdriver, a couple of doctors, a Scientologist in his goofy military uniform on leave from the big blue church down the street. Zalika takes a gift-wrapped box from her purse and lays it on the counter.

"What's this?" I ask.

"A present, for being so kind," Zalika replies.

"Come on," I say.

"You don't know," she says. "Having you to talk to was important."

She's a nice person, and this is what nice people do.

"Well, thanks," I say. "Should I open it now?"

"No, no," she says quickly. "Wait until you get home."

She takes my hand again, squeezes it, then turns away.

"Good luck," she says as she walks out the door.

"Good luck to you," I reply.

★ ★ ★

I WALK HOME instead of taking the bus, which is like a crowded coffin at this time of day. The city is wide awake and all a-rumble. The Russian who owns the liquor store is hosing down the sidewalk. He smiles around his cigarette and directs the stream of water into the gutter so I can pass. A city maintenance crew is doing roadwork. The sound of the jackhammer makes my heart stutter behind my ribs. A hundred degrees by afternoon, the radio said. The start of a heat wave.

When I get back to the apartment, I sit at the little dining-room table with Zalika's gift in front of me. Distant explosions rattle the bedroom door. Troy's TV. I unwrap the box and open it. It's a watch, a nice Bulova. Stainless steel, tiny diamonds sparkling around the dial. I once lived in a world where men wore watches like this, but not anymore. The jackals around here would cut my arm off for it. I'll put it on eBay and bank the couple hundred bucks I get.

I want to show the watch to Troy, but he doesn't answer when I knock. Maybe he's already on his walk, left the History Channel blaring. I open the door a crack and peek in to make sure. He's lying on his back on the bed. His mouth is wide open, his eyes too.

"Troy," I call out. "Buddy."

He doesn't respond. On the TV a kamikaze plane plows into the deck of an aircraft carrier and disintegrates into smoke and flame and white-hot shrapnel.

★ ★ ★

A MASSIVE HEART attack. That's what Troy's parents tell me. He died in his sleep, they say, never knew what hit him. I hope that's true.

"He was doing so great," I say as I help his mom and dad box up his possessions. "Exercising, eating right, losing weight."

His mom is still suffering. She has to sit down every few minutes and fight back tears. I overheard her telling her husband how disgusting this place is. Pomp and Circumstance, Troy called them. His dad once asked him not to come home for Thanksgiving because seeing him so fat would make the other guests uncomfortable.

"I hope you told him to fuck off," I said.

Troy shrugged. "They're a little confused," he said.

I only knew him for four months, and if his parents had asked, I wouldn't have been able to tell them much about his life. His favorite food was pizza. He enjoyed war movies and old TV game shows. I don't think he was ever serious about moving to Berlin and marrying that girl, but I think he liked thinking he was. He could hold his liquor. He didn't believe in God.

I GIVE TROY'S ghost a week to clear out before I begin to sleep in the bedroom. Just when I start to worry how I'm going to make rent, Best Buy calls. They put me in personal electronics, but inside of a month I'm in charge of the computer department. It's enough for me to pay my bills, eat out once in a while, and give Edward and Star some gas money for their drive back to Florida.

Both my kids e-mail me on my birthday, Kyle a cartoon of five fat pink pigs farting out "Happy Birthday," Gwennie a little note addressed to Dear Old Dad. I call their mother and update her on my situation. She's happy to hear I'm getting my act together but still hems and haws when I ask if she'll let me see the children if I come to Utah.

"All I'm asking is that you think about it," I say.

"I will," she says.

I take a beer down to the pool. The swatch of night sky overhead is a livid purple, too bright for stars. Lights are blazing inside the apartments on both floors of the complex, and all around me people are settling in after a long day. They eat dinner, watch TV, talk to friends. It feels good to be in the middle of it.

One year ago tonight I was squatting in the basement of an abandoned house near Dodger Stadium with an old junkie named Tom Dirt. He'd picked up a check from the VA and managed to cash it without identification, and the money was burning a hole in his pocket. His knee was giving him trouble, so he said if I'd fly, he'd buy. I went to see my man and returned with a little tar for Tom and a fat rock for me.

We sat on a couple of filthy mattresses and got ourselves to where we needed to be by the only light we had, a few flickering candles that threw crazy shadows that kept me jumping.

Tom jerked out of a nod at one point and shouted, "Merry Christmas!"

"It's not Christmas," I said. "It's my birthday."

"Okay, so happy birthday," Tom said, and coughed into his fist so long and so hard, I thought he was done for.

But he lived on, and so did I. Jesus fuck, it's a mystery, all of it. Smoke a cigarette, change the channel, stare into space. Then go to sleep, go to work, and come home again, over and over and over, until all your questions are answered or you forget you ever wondered.

TO ASHES

PAPÁ GETS HOME FROM work at six and tells Miguel and his little brother, Francisco, to turn off the Xbox and put on the news. Miguel glances at Francisco with raised eyebrows, like, *What's up with that?*, because the old man normally heads right for the shower to wash off the sweat and plaster dust before the family has dinner.

The newscaster is talking about a wildfire that's burning out of control east of San Diego. Papá shoos Miguel and Francisco off the couch and sits in front of the TV, leaning forward to watch intently. Mamá pokes her head in from the kitchen, a worried look on her face, and Miguel can tell she's freaked too by the change in routine.

"What's going on?" she says.

"A fire at the border," Papá replies.

Mamá walks into the living room, a dish towel twisted in her hands. "And so?"

"Alberto and Maria are crossing tonight."

Alberto is Miguel's cousin, Papá's nephew. Maria is his wife. They live in the village outside Durango where Papá

213

was born, a place so small it doesn't even have a name. Papá drags the whole family down there every couple of years for a visit, trips Miguel dreads because it's hot and dirty, and the food sucks, and the only bathroom is an out-house buzzing with flies. Alberto is cool, though. He let Miguel ride his motorcycle last time they were there and took them swimming in the river. He's only a year older than Miguel but already married, and Miguel has heard Papá say that he was thinking of coming to the U.S.

A map flashes onscreen, the location of the fire. Papá points. "El Chango's trail is right there," he says. "He'll bring them that way."

The sound of the front door opening makes Miguel jump. Carmen comes in from cheerleading practice and sees everyone staring at the TV. "What's going on?" she says in English.

Mamá shushes her, and Papá turns up the sound. This must be some serious shit, because nothing ever gets to the old man. All he does is work and sleep, barely saying five words most days. Miguel watches him watch TV and is suddenly a little scared.

Everybody tries to act normal at dinner. They pass around the chicken and rice and listen to Carmen and Francisco bicker. But that right there is weird; Papá would normally shut them down with a look. Instead, he's lost in thought, barely eating anything, big gristly fists clenched on either side of his plate. Miguel imitates Don Cheto, the funny guy on the radio, hoping to get a smile out of him, but no, nothing.

Later, while Miguel, Carmen, and Francisco are doing their homework at the dining-room table, Papá makes a phone call in the bedroom. When he reappears and sits on the couch, Mamá rushes in from the kitchen to ask what he found out. Miguel leans back in his chair so he can hear what they're saying.

"They left Durango last week and met with El Chango in Tijuana," Papá says. "Everything was in order, and they were supposed to call Rosa after crossing." He's talking about Aunt Rosa, his sister in San Diego. "She hasn't heard from them yet."

"Maybe they turned back," Mamá says. "Maybe *la migra* got them."

Papá shrugs. "Maybe."

Francisco leans over and whispers to Miguel from behind his hand: "Are they dead?"

"You're so fucking stupid," Miguel whispers back, reaching out to flick the kid's ear.

Francisco doesn't yell or tattle or throw a fit. Even he knows this isn't a night for those kinds of antics. Instead, he gets up and walks into the living room and puts his arms around Mamá's waist and buries his face in her blouse. Miguel turns back to his homework but can't concentrate. His mind is full of hungry flames that devour the equations before he can solve them.

THE COP SHOWS up at dawn, a stocky woman with a man's haircut. Brewer is half awake when she pounds on the door of his trailer. He's sweating in bed after a restless night, his mind drifting between past and present. His dead mother makes pancakes while "How Much Is That Doggie in the Window?" plays on an old radio, but at the same time he smells smoke from the fire that glows brighter on the horizon than the rising sun.

"Mr. Brewer," the cop calls, banging again.

"Give me a minute," Brewer growls.

He sits on the edge of the mattress. His shoulder hurts, his knees, and pulling on a pair of jeans is all kinds of painful. He shakes a Marlboro from the pack on the nightstand and puts a match to it as he limps to the door.

"Morning," the cop says when he opens up. She's the same one who came by yesterday talking about mandatory evacuations, but Brewer knows the law: they can't force him to go; all they can do is warn him. This land, ten acres of scrub hard by the border, is the only thing his dad left him, the only thing he has left, so he's decided to make a stand.

"You're up bright and early," he says to the cop.

"I was worried about you," she replies. "The fire's less than a mile west of here now and burning this way. I thought I could talk you into packing some stuff, and I'll lead you out."

Brewer steps into the yard to see for himself the smoke rising over the hills and rolling slowly toward him. The sight dries his mouth and sets his hands to trembling, but he has to trust that the preparations he's made will enable him to ride out the blaze. He's cut back the chaparral to create a firebreak around the trailer, sprayed retardant on the remaining shrubs, and hooked up heavy-duty hoses to all his spigots.

"I'll be fine," he says to the cop.

"This is the last time I'll be passing by, and the fire crews are pulling back to the 94, so they won't be coming either," she says. "You'll be on your own."

I've always been on my own, he wants to tell her, but that'll just sound dramatic. Cassius, the skinny stray that showed up a few years ago and never left, trots out of the trailer and sniffs the air, then walks over and stares up at Brewer with a worried look. The mutt was old when he arrived and is even older now, with white hair on his muzzle and a milky cataract in one eye.

Brewer reaches down to scratch the animal's ears and asks the cop, "Will you take my dog?"

"Can't," she says. "It's against regulations."

"Well, you might as well be on your way, then. Someone must need you somewhere."

The cop heads back to her truck but stops before reaching it and turns like she's going to try once more to get Brewer to leave. As soon as she opens her mouth to speak, she inhales a bit of floating ash and begins to cough. After a couple of attempts to say what she was going to say, she gives up, throws Brewer a little wave, and, still coughing, climbs into her truck and drives away.

Brewer smiles to himself. She's actually not bad for a cop. Big old bull dyke looks like she might even be able to hold her own in a fight.

The wind has come up, and ash swirls in the air like a light snow, dusting the hood of Brewer's pickup, the leaves of the rosebush, the surface of the water in the dog's bowl. Brewer can see flames now, for the first time, bright orange banners fluttering through the smoke.

He walks into the trailer and retrieves *The Complete Works of William Shakespeare* from the table in the dining nook, the same battered copy he's hauled around most of his life, ever since he realized there was more truth in one of those plays than in the entire Holy Bible. Most of his days still start with a cup of coffee and the book, him opening it at random in search of some bit of wisdom to chew on, so it'll be the only thing he takes with him if he winds up running.

He carries the book out to the truck, then ties a bandanna around his nose and mouth, pulls on a pair of ski goggles, and picks up a hoe. Cassius follows him to the firebreak, a ten-foot-wide strip Brewer has scraped down to dirt, a kind of moat surrounding the trailer. The dog lolls in a patch of shade while Brewer attacks a manzanita bush, widening the break even more. His hands are already covered with blisters from the work he's done over the past twenty-four hours, and his back is killing him, but he can't just sit and wait for the fire to get here. He's let too many things run him over like that in the past.

When he pauses to empty the sweat pooled inside his goggles, he notices that the flames have moved closer and that the smoke has gone from black to pink as the sun has risen. A fire department plane on its way to drop the load of water it has in its belly onto the blaze roars low over-head, and Cassius sends up a pitiful howl.

"What are you bawling about?" Brewer yells at the dog, then blows his nose into his bandanna. The snot comes out black, and when he spits, that's black too.

MIGUEL WATCHES MAMÁ while he eats his Froot Loops. She's making bacon-and-egg burritos for him and Papá to take with them. Papá sits across the table, sipping a cup of milky coffee. The old man shook Miguel awake half an hour ago and told him to get dressed, they were going to look for Alberto and Maria.

"What about school?" Miguel asked, but all Papá said was "Don't wake your brother."

The old man is bringing him along to translate. After all these years, he understands English pretty well but still can't speak it. Hearing him try embarrasses Miguel. At Home Depot or the DMV or on parent-teacher night Miguel bites his tongue when the old man struggles to put together a few awkward sentences, then steps in and talks over him at the first sign of confusion on the face of whomever he's addressing.

"You have to let him try," Mamá always says afterward. "How else will he learn?"

"It's easier if I do it," Miguel replies. "People don't have all day."

Mamá wraps the burritos in aluminum foil and slides them into a plastic grocery bag. Papá looks up from his cof-fee and smiles at her.

"Don't worry," he says.

She shakes her head in reply, tight-lipped, her eyes puffy. Miguel realizes she's been crying.

"I'll take good care of your baby," Papá continues. "I promise."

A bit worried himself, Miguel asks Papá how he plans to find Alberto and Maria.

"You just do as I say," the old man snaps.

When Papá comes to a decision, he sticks to it no matter what, putting all his pride behind it, and this stubbornness makes Miguel uneasy. He remembers the time the old man took him and Francisco fishing in a friend's boat. They motored far out into the ocean, and the weather suddenly turned bad. Dark clouds crashed into one another overhead, and the tiny boat was rocked by wind-whipped waves. The frightened boys began to cry and begged Papá to turn back.

"Don't you trust your father?" he shouted. "I know what I'm doing."

He didn't, not at all, and they ended up running out of fuel and nearly capsizing before another boat picked them up. To this day the old man won't admit they were in any danger. When he tells the story, it's only to joke about how scared the boys were. But he was scared too. Miguel saw it in his eyes when the engine stopped and when the lightning flashed, and he heard it in his voice as he recited a prayer under his breath.

When Miguel walks out the front door of the house a few minutes later, Papá is checking the oil in his truck in preparation for the trip. "Did you bring a coat?" the old man says.

Miguel holds up his letterman's jacket. He's doing varsity track this year and is close to breaking the school record in long jump. A couple more inches, one good trip off the board, and he'll have it. Mosco, the family's Chihuahua, barks at him and bounces around his legs.

"Don't let him out," Mamá calls through the bars covering the living-room window. The yellow stucco on the house is crisscrossed with gray patches where Papá has repaired cracks. He keeps saying he's going to repaint but never finds the time. Mamá has had enough of his promises and calls the house the Pride of El Monte just to piss him off.

Miguel holds the dog back with his foot while he steps through the gate in the waist-high chain-link fence, then quickly yanks his shoe away and slams the gate shut. He walks to the truck and climbs in on the passenger side. The burritos on the seat beside him give off a greasy smell that fills the cab.

He's going to miss a history quiz and track practice today, but what's most fucked is that he was supposed to cut sixth period and sneak with Michelle to her cousin's apartment, where she swore she'd finally give it up after a whole month of dry-humping and hand jobs. It'd be his first time getting laid, something he's been thinking about since he was, like, twelve. And Michelle is fine, too, not like Lydia, that beast his homey Rigo got with last year and still brags about. Fucking Papá is going to ruin everything.

The old man slides behind the wheel and starts the truck. He raises his hand to Mamá, and she raises hers to him. Miguel puts in his earbuds and turns on his music. As soon as they graduate, he and Rigo are moving to Tucson to work as trainers at Rigo's uncle's gym. Michelle might come too. He can't wait.

He sleeps most of the way down to Tijuana and even when he's awake pretends he isn't so that he doesn't have to talk to the old man. They park on the American side of the border in a dirt lot next to a currency-exchange place. Papá hands him one of the burritos and unwraps another for himself, and they eat sitting on the tailgate of the truck. A battered train rolls past, its boxcars covered with graffiti, both Spanish and English: *El Solitario, Led Zeppelin, Kim is the shit.*

The walk to the crossing is a short one, past the McDonald's and the trolley stop, up and over a bridge spanning the freeway. Soon Miguel is pushing through the turnstile in the tall iron fence separating the two countries, and, just like that, the cars are dustier, the pigeons rattier, the music louder.

Papá goes to a taxi stand and negotiates with a driver, a fat dude in a cowboy hat. Miguel has trouble keeping up with what's being said. His Spanish has never been very good, and he forgets a little more each year. The driver leads them to an empty cab, and the old man sits in front and tells Miguel to get in back. The fat dude climbs in and taps his horn twice at the other drivers lounging at the stand before squeezing into the traffic headed into town.

★　　　★　　　★

THE FIRE REACHES Brewer's place around nine. It barrels down the hill fronted by a twenty-foot wall of flame. The dry grass hisses as it burns, and the oily shrubs explode, sending up showers of flaming shrapnel. The willows and cottonwoods lining the creek that runs along the western edge of the property wither and go from green to orange to black.

Brewer stands at the break in goggles and bandanna, hose in one hand, rake in the other. His eyes sting from the smoke, and it's impossible to draw a deep breath without coughing. The heat increases as the fire pushes closer, and the exposed flesh on his forehead feels tight enough to tear.

If he thinks of all of it at once, pauses to acknowledge the intensity of the blaze, the heat, the choking smoke, he'll cut and run, he knows it, and die in a futile scramble for safety. So instead he focuses on individual flames and wayward sparks, moving from task to task, head down, humming that damn song, the one about the doggie.

An ember sails across the break on a gust of wind and lands in a clump of dead weeds. Brewer drags the hose over and douses the flare-up, then spots another and soaks that too. He replaces the doggie song with Hamlet's soliloquy "To be or not to be..." Not his favorite speech, not his favorite play, but something he memorized as a young man because even the roughnecks he worked with in the oil fields recognized it as something fine and would reward him with whiskey and backslaps when he stood, deliriously drunk, and recited it in those long-ago jukebox honky-tonks that were their only respite from day upon hellish day on the rigs.

He's up to "the rub" when a sage bush inside the perimeter catches fire and ignites a mat of brittle grass that stretches all the way over to where his truck is parked. By the time he pulls the hose into position, the ground beneath the vehicle is on fire. His legs shake as he squeezes the pistol-gripped nozzle and aims the stream of water at the flames. Two of the truck's tires explode, but he manages to extinguish the blaze before it does any more damage.

A step back, a clattery breath, and out of the corner of his eye he sees that the old oak that shades the trailer, a tree he should have cut down years ago, *would have* if he hadn't been moved by its gnarled dignity, is suddenly aflame. He's soaked its branches half a dozen times since hearing of the approaching fire, but the air itself is thirsty in this parched place, so, despite his precautions, the tree is dropping burning leaves onto his home.

He climbs onto the picnic table next to the trailer and sprays the roof and the branches above it, which are laced with orange flame. He's making progress, but then a blazing limb gives way with a loud crack and crashes down onto the trailer.

Brewer hops off the table and retrieves the rake. He hooks the limb with the tool and yanks repeatedly in an effort to dislodge it. The stubborn tangle of smoldering branches comes loose all of a sudden, throwing him off balance, and he falls backward and brings the limb down on top of himself. He scrabbles wildly to get free of the burning cage, then snags the limb with the rake and drags it across the yard.

The fire is lapping at the break on all sides now, and the intense heat ripples the air, giving the blaze the ghostly quality of something seen through an old, warped windowpane. Thick, black smoke rolls over Brewer in choking waves, and the sharp pop and crackle of flames chewing through the chaparral plucks at his nerves. He opens his mouth to yell, to prove he's still here, but only a ragged cough comes out.

Next time, I let it burn, he thinks, and staggers toward a new flare-up that's bloomed inside the perimeter.

PAPÁ AND THE taxi driver talk like old friends as they zip past concrete-and-cinder-block dental clinics, auto-repair shops, and twenty-four-hour pharmacies. All the buildings look like they're either half finished or on their way to falling down, and music blasts out of every open door. A man in a dirty chicken suit dances in front of a restaurant, beckoning passing cars.

The stink of burning trash in the air makes Miguel nauseous. Or maybe he's carsick. He tries concentrating on the CD dangling from the rearview mirror of the cab, watches it twirl and flash, but that only makes him feel worse.

They turn off the pavement onto a deeply rutted dirt road that leads up a steep hill past shacks pieced together out of cardboard and corrugated tin, scavenged wood and plastic tarps. It's even more pitiful than Durango. Look at the garbage piled in the street. Look at the women washing clothes in a muddy stream. *Vatos* with tattooed faces bend to peer into the taxi as it passes, and the driver locks the doors.

The cab stops in front of a house that's a little nicer than the rest, with four solid walls and glass in the windows. A satellite dish perches on the roof like a vulture, and a new gas grill takes up most of the dirt yard. Papá climbs out and knocks on the door. A woman clutching a naked baby answers and talks briefly with the old man, stepping outside to point down the road.

The cabdriver turns in his seat to address Miguel. "You like L.A.?" he asks in English.

"It's okay," Miguel replies.

"I live there ten years," the driver says. "I like the money, but Mexico is better for me."

Miguel doesn't understand how that could possibly be.

Papá returns to the cab and tells the driver to go to the end of the street and make a left. They stop again, in front of a windowless concrete building with a Corona logo painted on the side.

"Cuidado," the driver says when Papá gets out of the cab. Careful. Miguel gets out too, because he'd rather be with his father than the driver if something goes wrong.

The only light inside the building comes from a dozen strands of Christmas bulbs strung across the ceiling. Their blinking reveals a glass-doored refrigerator stocked with beer and a wooden shelf lined with bottles of tequila. The place is a cantina of some sort, judging by the white plastic tables and chairs scattered about. A little man in a red apron is sitting on an overturned bucket next to the refrigerator. He stands when Miguel and his father enter, his eyes full of questions.

The only customer is a dark-skinned drunk in sweatpants and a Chivas jersey who looks to be asleep in his chair.

"Chango," Papá calls out to him.

The drunk squints at the old man, drinks from a bottle of Modelo, then lets his chin drop to his chest again. Papá walks over and kneels beside him, grabs the arm of his chair, and shakes it.

"*¿Qué pasa?*" El Chango mumbles without lifting his head or opening his eyes.

The old man asks about Alberto and Maria, explains that they were supposed to cross last night. It's difficult for Miguel to hear what he's saying because he speaks so softly, almost whispering into the coyote's ear. A fly buzzing around the room is louder than he is.

El Chango frowns and shakes his head, eyes still closed. He reaches out and tries to push the old man away. Papá's face hardens into a mask Miguel has never seen before. "Listen," he says. "You know El Teo, right?"

The name is a mystery to Miguel, but El Chango has heard it. He opens his little red eyes and looks Papá up and down.

"You better talk to me, or you'll soon be talking to him," the old man says.

El Chango grunts and licks his thick lips. He tugs at his jersey and has another sip of beer. "We set out at dusk," he begins, then slurs out the story of how he led Alberto, Maria, and two other *pollos,* young boys, across the border and up into the scrubby hills of the U.S. side. He knew about the fire, could see the orange glow of it in the distance as they trudged along, but that seemed to him a good thing. The border patrol would be forced to pull back, and the crossing would be an easy one.

The wind, though, fuck, who can predict that? It changed in an instant and sent the flames racing toward them. El Chango hurried the *pollos* along, but the pregnant girl slowed them down. When the smoke thickened and sparks began to fall like burning rain, the group insisted they turn around. El Chango climbed to the top of a hill and looked back the way they'd come to see if this was an option, and, Mother of God, he couldn't believe his eyes: a sea of fire now blocked any retreat.

There was nothing to do but keep moving, try to stay in front of the flames. This proved to be impossible. The fire moved too quickly and finally overtook them in a steep, narrow canyon, roaring and spitting like some bright, burning beast. El Chango lost his nerve. He and the boys abandoned the pregnant girl and her husband and sprinted up the path, not stopping until they no longer felt heat on the backs of their necks. Upon reaching the railroad tracks that cut across the desert there, they sat and waited for over an hour, but nobody else appeared out of the inferno.

El Chango hangs his head and weeps when he finishes.

Miguel is embarrassed by the tears. He hasn't cried in years and is sure he never will again. He stares at the Modelo bottle as the man sobs. The Christmas lights turn it red, then green, then blue.

Papá pulls a map from his pocket and thrusts it at the coyote, demanding he show him where they crossed. El Chango wipes his eyes with his palms, squints down at the map and points to a remote area east of Tecate.

"The same trail as always?" Papá asks.

El Chango nods.

"Okay, then, let's go," Papá says to Miguel, and for once Miguel is happy to obey one of his orders.

BREWER SITS AT the picnic table and drinks a celebratory beer. His property lies charred and smoldering all around him, but he's saved the trailer and the truck, the pump house and the propane tank. Not finding much fuel here, the fire passed through quickly and is now crawling toward Calexico and Mexicali. The smoke has cleared, except for a few white snakes still writhing over shrubs that haven't yet burned themselves out.

Brewer's hands were slightly scorched fighting the fire. He rests a plastic bag filled with ice on the blistered skin. His eyebrows are gone too, burned away, and some of his hair, but nothing that won't grow back. All in all he's proud of having stood his ground.

"Cassius," he shouts. "Get your ass out here."

He last saw the dog cowering under the trailer right before the fire descended upon them. A tickle of worry makes him bend to peer into the animal's hiding place.

"Cassius?" he calls again, but detects no movement in the shadows.

He tells himself the mutt is fine. Probably holed up somewhere else on the property, still too frightened by the smoke and flames to come out. He forces his mind to move on. There are plenty of other issues to be dealt with. The power is out, for example, and since it might be days before repairs are made, he decides dinner tonight will be the T-bone he's been saving in the freezer, with ice cream for dessert. He's in the middle of a mental inventory of the rest of the contents of the refrigerator, dividing it into stuff that will spoil and stuff that won't, when a watery uneasiness once again creeps up on him.

"Cassius?" he shouts, before finally figuring out what's bothering him: No birds. They've all disappeared in the wake of the fire, and the quiet is unsettling. No ravens bitching, no doves courting. No finches, no jays, no quail. There's only the wind now, and the distant whine of an engine coming closer. Brewer cranes his neck to look down the road and sees a cloud of dust. Probably the lady cop, expecting the worst. Won't she be surprised. He stands and tucks in his shirt, straightens his collar.

But it's not the cop who drives into the yard, it's the Sharp brothers, a pair of former marines who still favor high-and-tights and camo. They live near Lake Morena with their wives and kids, get by as handymen, and, under the mantle of patriotism, spend their spare hours patrolling the border in search of illegals. The deal is, they're not allowed to detain the wetbacks or confront them in any way, only to radio their location to the border patrol, but Brewer suspects there's some wink-wink nudge-nudge going on around that.

Steve is behind the wheel of the Jeep, Matthew in the passenger seat. The only way Brewer can tell them apart is that Steve has tattoos and Matthew doesn't. Nice enough guys, but he isn't looking to get any friendlier with them than he already is. He can't help wondering about the essential qualities of folks who get their kicks fucking with the poor and desperate.

"You made it!" Steve shouts.

"I wasn't sure for a while there," Brewer says. "Goddamn thing almost seemed to have a grudge. How'd it go at your place?"

"No problems," Matthew says. "The crews kept it south of the 94."

"So everybody got lucky. Good. Say, you didn't happen to see that old dog that hangs around here on your way in, did you?"

"Nope," Steve says. "He run off?"

"No, no," Brewer says. "I just haven't seen him in an hour or so. Where you guys off to?"

"Ah, you know, looking for trouble," Steve says. There's a scorpion on his neck, and rattlesnakes coil up both arms.

"The coyotes are for sure gonna take advantage of the fire," Matthew says. "They'll be bringing across as many *pollos* as they can while everyone's busy."

Brewer notices a couple of shotguns in the backseat of the Jeep, and each man has a Glock on his hip. A bit excessive for "observers," but then again, Brewer can't imagine that vigilantes like Matthew and Steve are too popular out there in no-man's-land.

"Well, take it easy," he says.

"You good?" Matthew says.

Brewer has two ruined tires on his truck and only one spare, but he'll worry about that tomorrow, walk up the road to where he can get a signal on his phone or hitch into Calexico. It's always been like that: If he can do for himself, he will.

"I'm good," he says.

Steve backs the Jeep out and whips it around toward a dirt track that leads to the border, and Brewer is suddenly beat all the way down to his bones. He calls for Cassius a few more times, then walks to the trailer and pulls himself up the step to get inside. Everything hurts when he lies on the bed, everything's against him. Not even a bird left to sing him to sleep.

THE LITTLE TOWN of Campo is full of fire trucks, and firefighters in helmets and heavy coats wander in and out of a convenience store and commiserate in the parking lot under a sun made sickly by a pall of ashy smoke. More smoke roils in grubby billows on the horizon.

A highway patrolman manning a checkpoint steps out into the road in front of Papá's truck and waves him to a stop. He asks to see identification, and Papá hands over his green card and driver's license. The cop bends to peer in the window at Miguel and says, "You too."

Miguel slides his California ID out of his wallet. Anger and embarrassment keep him from looking the cop in the eye. The guy is barking at them like they're a couple of wetbacks. He shuffles through the cards, examining them perfunctorily, then passes them back.

"*¿Habla inglés?*" he says.

"I do," Miguel replies.

"The road ahead is closed because of the fire," the cop says. "You have to go back the way you came." He makes a chopping motion with his hand. "*No más* driving. *Fuego.*"

Miguel translates for Papá, who mumbles "I understand" in Spanish and backs the truck up. They turn around and drive maybe a half mile before the old man pulls over at a wide spot in the road and shuts off the engine. Miguel's heart sinks when Papá steps out of the truck, grabbing a red fleece jacket and the bag containing the rest of the burritos.

"We'll walk," he says.

"For real?" Miguel says. He'd hoped the old man had given up and that they'd be back in L.A. in time for his rendezvous with Michelle.

"Bring your coat," Papá says.

Miguel clutches his letterman's jacket to his chest. "No way. It'll get messed up."

"Why did I pay so much money for it if you're not going to wear it?"

"Not out here," Miguel says.

Papá hisses angrily and walks back to open the toolbox in the bed of the truck. He pulls out a couple of plastic bottles of Coke, drops them into the bag with the burritos, and sets off in the direction of Campo, expecting Miguel to follow. Miguel wonders what would happen if he didn't, but then jogs to catch up.

"Do you even know where we're going?" he asks.

"A road up here leads to the border," Papá says. "We'll start there."

A hundred yards farther an overgrown jeep trail shoots off to the south, not much more than tire tracks worn into the hardpan. Miguel and the old man follow it over a series of low, scrub-covered hills and down into a sandy wash that then becomes their path for a time. When they finally clamber out of the gulley and onto a rocky knob with a view of the surrounding terrain, Miguel pulls up short, shocked by what he sees.

The fire-ravaged wasteland in front of him extends all the way to the horizon, a nightmare landscape of blackened chaparral and still smoldering oaks. Ash swirls in the hot wind, whipping around the charred skeletons of manzanita and sage bushes and newly exposed boulders that thrust up from the scorched plain like broken teeth.

Miguel watches a trio of buzzards circle in the hazy sky above the burn zone, then drop suddenly and disappear. Going after a dead rabbit. A dead deer. Worse. Papá's crazy. They'll never find Alberto and Maria alive. If the two of them were out here when the fire passed through, they're nothing but smoke now.

"Papá," Miguel begins, ready to say what he's thinking, but the old man cuts him off with a wave of his hand.

"We're going on," he says.

Miguel can't believe how stupid this is, but it's no use trying to reason with him. The guy can barely read, and his writing looks like a little kid's. He still believes in ghosts and good-luck charms and still gets on his knees every night to pray. *Puro* Durango, man, *puro naco*. He passes Miguel a Coke and tells him to drink. Miguel drains the bottle and tosses it out into the devastation. *Tucson,* he thinks. *Eyes on the prize.*

The old man pulls up the neck of his T-shirt to cover his nose and mouth, and they set off across the burned desert. Miguel's shuffling feet raise a plume of dust that drags behind them like a tail, and he hopes the border patrol notices it and forces them to turn around. If they're still following a trail, Miguel can't see it, so he watches the old man's back, goes where he goes.

Fifteen minutes later they reach the border fence, a ten-foot-high barrier constructed of panels of corrugated steel, Mexico on the far side, the U.S. over here. They stand on the wide dirt road that fronts the fence, and Papá points out where someone has burrowed beneath the panels to create a series of tight passages between the two countries, shallow depressions worn smooth by all the bodies that have squeezed through them.

"Those are El Chango's," he says.

"Is that how you came across?" Miguel asks.

"Sometimes."

Miguel would ask what he means by this but knows he won't get an answer. Papá never talks about his past beyond the few stories he tells of growing up poor, stories that are supposed to make Miguel and his siblings feel lucky for all the things they have. Miguel knows the old man moved to L.A. when he was twenty, met Mamá the next year, and had him a year later. There are photos of all that in Mamá's albums. And he knows the old man lived in TJ for a while before that.

"What did you do there?" Miguel once asked him.

"What everyone did," Papá replied, and that was all Miguel could pry out of him.

The wind picks up and whistles through the gaps in the fence. The old man points to a burned hill on the U.S. side and says, "That way."

Miguel spits, hikes up his baggy jeans, and again follows his father into the desert. If he'd known they were going to be hiking around out here all goddamn day, he'd have worn a belt.

SEVENTY YEARS OLD. Someone, some kid, taunts Brewer with this in a dream: "You're seventy, man." Brewer denies it, but it's true. Born July 5, 1944, in Licking Springs, Missouri. Henry Brewer Jr., only son of Henry and Jan Brewer. Born at home because they couldn't afford a hospital, and no money is also why they left Missouri soon afterward, staggering west.

Dad loved movies—could quote the stars and sing the

songs, could laugh or cry on cue—so Hollywood was the goal. It took ten years to get there, with stops in Tulsa and Houston, Denver and Phoenix, that place in New Mexico with the wasps' nest, a dusty motel in Vegas. Dad sold cars to pay the bills, sold houses, sold hamburgers. The man could sell anything. He had the right smile, the right spirit. And Mom was his little helper, always there with an encouraging word and a hug, always ready to unpack when they hit town and load up again when it was time to move on.

Brewer? Well, he figured out early on that he was just along for the ride, one more item to be checked off the list before they drove away: keys returned, car gassed up, boy in backseat. If he ever resented this, he can't remember. These days, the past seems like a fuse that was lit the moment he was born, one that now burns faster than he can run.

What he does know is that Hollywood didn't work out and Dad never got any closer to the movies than buying a ticket every Saturday. But that was fine because Mom kept right on ironing his shirts and laughing at his jokes and rubbing his head when it hurt, saying, "Do that thing from *Gunga Din* again." They were more in love than any couple Brewer has ever known, and they barely noticed when he joined the navy at eighteen and moved away for good.

Out of spite he went the other way across the country: Phoenix and Dallas, Gulfport and Miami. He didn't have Dad's charm, so he had to get his hands dirty. He put in twelve-hour days in factories and on oil rigs, pounded nails and welded steel. And he didn't have Mom to come home to either. There were women, sure, and men, but nothing that lasted. As soon as anyone opened up, he panicked. Their secrets and sadnesses were like a layer of grease on his skin, rank and suffocating. He always felt best driving away from the last place and toward the next one.

He only brushed up against love once: New Orleans, 1969. A bartender named Charlie Wiggins. He'd have come off the road for that boy if such a thing were conceivable back then. They were friends, lovers, one soul in two bodies, flesh the only wall between them. Charlie liked Shakespeare too. They'd get drunk and read the plays together, the big death scenes—Romeo and Mercutio, Othello and Desdemona—and both end up weeping. An idyll like that can't last, however. There's a law somewhere. An icy road, a sudden curve, a tree—that's how Charlie went.

And then time flew. The men around Brewer married and had kids and grandkids. They Christmas-shopped and mowed lawns and cried at their daughters' weddings. Brewer opens his eyes and stares at the wall of the trailer. Seventy years old. He was vain when he was younger, too proud of his strong arms, his handsome face, his thick cock. But all that's gone now. Damn the quivering jowls and sagging belly, damn the muscles that ache for no reason. He was also proud of his solitude, how even in a crowded room he was still somehow so beautifully alone. And now? Well, he's still alone, but now he's lonely too, lonely like never before. So also damn the heart that can't forget.

Oh hell, he scolds himself. *Get up, old woman. You fought for this life this morning, now get up and finish living it.*

★　　★　　★

PAPÁ RECALLS THE general direction of El Chango's route, but the trail itself has been obliterated by the fire. Miguel follows the old man up one rocky hill, then another, then another. When they crest the third, Papá turns to look at where they've been, points to the first hill, and says, "That one. I'm sure of it now. We have to go back."

Frustrated protests boil up in Miguel's throat, but he falls in behind his father without a word. He'll drop dead before he complains again. He's as tough as the old man, tougher even. Younger, stronger. He plods along in his father's wake, his mind a hateful whirl. His feet hurt, and the dust makes him cough, but he's determined to outlast the old man and laugh in his face when he finally stalls.

They reach the top of the first hill again, almost an hour wasted. Papá crouches on top and squints at the smoking horizon in search of landmarks that have escaped the flames. Miguel is sure it's hopeless. Everything around them has burned. After a minute or so, though, the old man stands and points out a notch in a ridge up ahead.

"There," he says.

Bullshit; he's lost. But Miguel follows him silently. They descend and walk toward the ridge. Fifteen minutes. Twenty. The rhythmic *crunch crunch* of their footsteps is hypnotic, and Miguel has visions of Michelle naked and of all the shit he's seen in pornos that he wants to do to her. He almost bumps into his father when the old man stops suddenly and raises his hand.

Something big and black is lying on the ground in front of them, the burned carcass of an animal. Something horned and hooved. A shimmering blanket of flies peels away as they approach, revealing gory rents in the leathery flesh where other animals have already begun to feed. Miguel averts his eyes, and they make a wide detour around the remains.

Miguel asks for a drink, and Papá hands him the last bottle of Coke. There's barely any left.

"Is that it?" Miguel says.

Papá looks up at the sun, then down at his watch. "Another hour," he says. "After that we'll turn back."

A few minutes later, as they're making their way across a plain dotted with thickets of charred chaparral, Papá stumbles and goes down hard. He pops to his feet quickly, ignoring Miguel's outstretched hand, but grimaces and almost falls again as soon as he puts weight on his right ankle.

Miguel helps him sit, then watches as he unlaces and removes his paint-spattered work boot. The ankle has already begun to swell, and when Miguel moves the foot, the old man endures it, but with gritted teeth.

"Son of a bitch," he mutters under his breath.

Miguel stands and pulls his phone from his pocket. No signal.

"I'm going up there," he says, pointing at the ridge. "To call 911."

"No," Papá says. "I'm fine." He holds a deep breath and yanks the boot past his ankle. When it's all laced up, he struggles to his feet. "Let's go," he says.

Miguel can see that he's in pain. Without a word he moves up beside his father and drapes the old man's arm around his neck.

"You're taller than me," Papá says, like he's never noticed before.

"Didn't take much," Miguel says.

The old man looks ridiculous when he grins, ash all over his face, sweat dripping off his nose. Miguel pulls his arm tighter and starts toward the ridge, forcing him to work to keep up.

The hot, dusty climb to the notch exhausts both of them. They rest on boulders when they get there, look down into the valley on the other side. The fire burned through here too—the ground is still smoking in places—but somehow a small patch of land was spared. A weathered trailer, an old truck, a couple of sheds, even a bit of green grass.

Miguel is thirsty. His tongue sticks to the roof of his mouth, and he's light-headed. He reaches into the plastic bag for the Coke bottle.

"I'm going for water," he announces.

"Wait," Papá says. "Let me think."

"What's there to think about?"

The old man squints at Miguel, hesitant, then stands and holds out his hand.

"I know what you're up to," he says. "You're not leaving me out here for the vultures."

★　　★　　★

BREWER IS ABOUT to set out in search of Cassius when he spies some sort of fire-spawned beast hobbling and scraping down the road toward his place. Two heads, three legs, filthy clothes, bloodshot eyes festering in blackened faces. It's a man and a boy, illegals who managed to escape the flames. The wets normally avoid Brewer's property, sneak on to use his faucets now and then. If these two are coming up the driveway in broad daylight, they must be in trouble.

Brewer picks up the machete he was using earlier to hack away burned brush. He feels a little safer with it in his hand.

"*Hola,*" he calls out.

The kid holds up an empty soda bottle. "Can we get some water?"

Brewer points to a spigot with the machete, and the kid walks to the faucet, leaving the man he's with to stand unsteadily on his own.

"Speak English?" Brewer says.

"I do," the kid replies. He twists the handle on the faucet and holds the bottle under the stream of water that gushes out.

"Picked a bad day to cross, didn't you?" Brewer says.

"Cross?" the kid says.

"The border."

"We're legal," the kid says, irritated. "We're looking for someone."

Maybe, maybe not. Regardless, the man is close to toppling over without the kid's support. Brewer motions him to the picnic table. "Have a seat."

The man shakes his head. "Is okay," he says.

"Come on, take a break," Brewer insists.

The man limps to the table. He sits facing outward on the bench, bows his head, and rubs his eyes with his palms, exhausted. The kid finishes filling the bottle and brings it to him. The man drinks deeply, then hands the bottle back to the kid.

"What happened to your foot?" Brewer asks the man.

He starts to speak, but the kid talks over him. "He sprained his ankle. Can we have more water?"

"Get as much as you want," Brewer says. "How long you been looking for whoever you're looking for?"

"My cousins," the kid says. "A few hours. The cops wouldn't let us drive any farther."

The man scolds the kid in Spanish, tells him to keep his mouth shut. The kid snaps off a retort before crouching at the faucet again.

"Your dad?" Brewer asks.

The kid nods grudgingly.

Brewer walks to the picnic table and holds out his hand. "Henry Brewer," he says.

"Armando Morales," the man replies. They shake, and Brewer turns to the kid.

"Henry Brewer," he says again.

"Miguel."

"Sorry I mistook you."

Miguel shrugs, doesn't reply.

Brewer scratches the silver stubble on his chin. Father and son way out here on some sort of rescue mission, searching for family. That kind of devotion makes you look back at your own record. He sits down with Armando at the table and asks where they're headed, has Miguel translate. Armando is reluctant to say, mumbling something about a canyon that Miguel has to ask him to repeat twice before he can put it into English.

"I know every canyon between here and Calexico," Brewer says. "Maybe I can help you out."

Armando is interested but still wary, and Brewer understands why. A gringo like him asking questions must set off all kinds of alarms.

So suddenly this Henry Brewer is all up in their business. Miguel'd like to tell him to fuck off, because he's pretty sure Papá was about to admit defeat and head back to the truck a few minutes ago, but now the old man is all revved up again, showing Mr. Brewer the map and making Miguel repeat El Chango's story of last night's crossing.

When Mr. Brewer goes into the trailer for a better map, Miguel reminds Papá what he said a while ago about one more hour. The old man lays into him, asks why he never thinks of anybody but himself. If that's true, Miguel wants to say, why isn't he home right now, hooking up with Michelle, instead of out here chasing ghosts around the desert?

Mr. Brewer comes out carrying three beers. He sets one on the table in front of Papá and offers one to Miguel. Miguel takes it without asking the old man if it's okay and walks over to look at a partially burned tree hanging over the trailer. Let the old man and Mr. Brewer see what kind of plan they can make without him translating.

"The canyon I think you're looking for is about two miles away," Mr. Brewer says.

"Okay," the old man says. "We go."

"Yeah, but that ankle."

Papá stomps his foot twice. "We go."

Miguel picks up a singed leaf from the ground and crumples it between his fingers. Dude lives like a caveman out here. It's hilarious. And this beer: fucking Natural Light, fucking welfare swill.

"I'll walk you there," Mr. Brewer says to Papá.

The old man is confused. He looks to Miguel for a translation.

"He wants to come with us," Miguel says.

"I was going out to try to find my dog anyway," Mr. Brewer says, pointing to a hiking pole and a knapsack containing a bottle of water and a windbreaker.

Papá sips his beer, thinking it over. Miguel can tell he's taken a liking to this fool and wants to believe that he knows what he's talking about. He's not surprised when, a few minutes later, the old man says, "Okay, but we go now."

Mr. Brewer disappears into the trailer again, then pokes his head out seconds later and calls for Miguel. "Take these to your dad," he says, handing over a set of aluminum crutches.

Miguel carries the crutches to the old man but holds them just out of his reach. "If this isn't the right canyon, we give up and go home," he says.

"Fine," Papá replies. "But you better show this man respect."

Ha, Miguel thinks. Old people are always talking about respect. They demand it from everybody but don't give it to anyone.

Papá tucks the crutches under his arms and takes a few tentative steps.

BREWER HAS HIKED this whole area, followed every jeep road, tried every trail. He doesn't play golf, doesn't care for casinos, so walking is how he uses up his days, how he wears himself out and earns his evening whiskey. Sometimes he thinks he quit working too soon. He slept soundly when he was on a job, never once woke at three a.m. with a hundred pounds of sadness resting on his chest.

He leads the way, calling for Cassius every so often, and Armando and the boy follow. Armando keeps a good pace on the crutches. The actual trail used by the coyotes zigzags through the hills and runs up and down brush-choked ravines, but since Brewer and the pair he's guiding aren't trying to avoid the authorities, they can walk the first mile on a good dirt road, to where the steep, rocky canyon Armando described climbs to the railroad tracks on the outskirts of Campo.

Brewer checks over his shoulder often to make sure the man and boy are keeping up, and after fifteen minutes hollers back, "Still with me?"

"Yes. Good," Armando replies.

The boy says nothing. He's not happy about traipsing around the desert and can't hide it. The disdainful looks he was giving his father back at the trailer would have led to blows between strangers. Brewer feels for the kid. When he was that age, Dad would tell one of his stolen jokes and Mom would laugh and Brewer would want to bite his tongue off. Their blood was like poison in his veins.

He stops for a second to sip water and consult the map. The sun long ago reached its peak and is now sliding swiftly toward the horizon. Armando and the boy will have to hurry if they're going to check the canyon and get out by dark.

The Sharp brothers' Jeep is blocking the road when they round a bend. Both men are outside the truck, Steve studying the burned landscape through a pair of binoculars, Matthew drinking a beer. Matthew spots them before Brewer can holler a greeting, and fear blanks his face. He draws his Glock and points it.

"Halt!"

"It's just me," Brewer says, waving his hiking pole over his head.

"Who's that with you?"

"A couple of friends."

Steve's pistol is out now too. The guns don't frighten Brewer, but the men holding them make him nervous. He ambles toward them, a big smile on his face.

"What is this, the OK Corral?" he says.

"Levante tus manos," Steve shouts at Armando and Miguel.

"Come on now," Brewer says, but the brothers ignore him. Steve orders Armando and Miguel to lie on the ground, facedown, and father and son do as they're told. Brewer reaches out to grab Matthew's arm as he steps out from behind the Jeep and moves toward the prone figures.

"You're over the line," Brewer says, but Matthew shakes off his hand and continues to advance, his gun swinging back and forth between Armando and Miguel. Brewer has to hold himself back from going after him, from ripping the Glock out of his hand and shoving it in his face to let him feel what it's like to be on that end of it.

Matthew bends over Armando and pats him down, then slides the man's wallet from his back pocket and flips it open.

"License and green card," he announces. "Looks legit." He fingers a bit of cash. "And something like twenty bucks."

"Leave it," Steve barks.

Miguel hands Matthew his ID. Matthew glances at it, then drops it into the dirt and walks back to Brewer and Steve. "I thought we might have a hostage situation," he says to Brewer.

"Is that so," Brewer replies.

"What are you all doing out here, with the fire and everything?"

"None of your fucking business," Brewer says. He turns to Armando and Miguel. "You can get up now."

The pair stand slowly, brushing dirt and ash off their clothes.

"What's got you sideways?" Steve says to Brewer.

Brewer doesn't answer. He motions to Armando and Miguel. "Let's go."

"Border patrol woulda done the same," Matthew says, holstering his gun.

Brewer touches Armando and Miguel on their backs as they pass by, a signal to hurry. Armando's crutches squeak rhythmically. He and the kid squeeze past the Jeep and keep walking. Brewer waits until they're on their way before starting down the road himself.

"Actually, you should be thanking us," Steve calls after him.

"Horseshit," Brewer says without turning around.

The fire burned hot here. Not even the blackened bones of the trees are still standing. It's as if a bomb exploded, leaving only scorched sand and bare rock. Brewer concentrates on this, the destruction, the smoke still billowing in the distance. He'll not pause to lament the cruelty of man. Better to keep running with that as a given.

MIGUEL'S FOOT HURTS, a blister on top of his little toe, and he's hungry too. He checks over his shoulder again, worried that the *pendejos* in the truck may be following, but the road is clear. It's funny: He's lived in the city all his life, and out here is the first place he's had a gun pulled on him.

They eventually leave the road for a trail that weaves through burned scrub oak and manzanita before depositing them at the mouth of a narrow canyon already deep in afternoon shadow. Papá and Mr. Brewer consult the map and agree that this is the route taken by El Chango.

"I'll go on with you," Mr. Brewer says. "Seeing as how I'm already out here."

"So let's hurry then," Miguel says, eager to get this over with. The men act like they don't even see the sun, a virulent orange through the smoke, sitting just a hand's width above the hills to the west. Miguel decides to lead the way to try to speed them up. He tightens the laces on his sneakers, blows a clot of black snot from his nose, and sets off.

The trail is a pale scar running up the middle of the canyon floor, and at first the going is easy, the route fairly level. But then the canyon narrows, and the trail begins to climb. Papá has a hard time of it. The crutches keep slipping, and he falls farther and farther behind. Mr. Brewer hangs back to help him, but Miguel stays out front, still hoping to set a good pace.

Everything in the canyon burned. The chaparral, the grass. Miguel bends to pick a stick up off the ground, and it crumbles in his hand. The trail eventually spits him out onto a sandy flat. The canyon dead-ends here, in a hundred-foot wall of rock, but the trail continues, zigzagging up the wall in a series of steep switchbacks. Miguel turns to check the men's progress just in time to see Papá go down on one knee and Mr. Brewer step forward to lift him to his feet. It's going to take them forever to climb out of here.

Miguel kicks at a pile of burned wood. Once, twice, three times. A blackened skull is dislodged and rolls across the flat. Miguel backs quickly away from the pile as he realizes that what he took for wood is bone. A leg that ends in a melted shoe. A clawlike hand. The canyon walls close in, and his mouth dries out. He turns and races down the trail toward Papá and Mr. Brewer, stumbling when he reaches them, falling and sliding painfully across the ground on hands and knees.

"They're up there," he says. "Dead."

"You sure?" Mr. Brewer asks.

Miguel nods.

The three of them make their way to the flat together. Miguel hangs back when Papá and Mr. Brewer approach the bones. He doesn't want to see them again. Papá tosses his crutches aside when he reaches the pile and kneels beside it, reaches out to run his fingers over the remains.

Miguel stares down canyon, following the trail back to its mouth. He imagines the fire funneling up toward Alberto and Maria, their fear when they realized they wouldn't be able to outrun it, their pain as the flames enveloped them. A shiver runs through him. He doesn't want to die. Ever.

The sky overhead is now a deep blue streaked with pink and orange, and the first stars flicker weakly against it like they might still go out. Papá and Mr. Brewer discuss what to do next. Mr. Brewer says he'll hike out by himself. He thinks he can reach the highway before full dark and bring back help. But Papá shakes his head when Miguel translates this.

"I'll bury them here," he says. "It's nobody's job but mine."

He sticks his finger down into his sock, fishes around, and comes up with a square of green paper, a hundred-dollar bill folded small. He holds it out to Mr. Brewer. "Thank this man for his help and tell him he has my gratitude," he says to Miguel. "Then tell him to go home. He's done enough."

Mr. Brewer pushes the money aside. "I'm staying," he says.

"Take it," Papá says in English. "Please."

"Let's get to work."

They go back and forth, but Mr. Brewer won't be swayed. Papá finally relents and puts the bill away. He picks up the bag containing the burritos and passes it to Miguel. "Share with him," he says, nodding at Mr. Brewer, then walks to a spot near the bones, kneels, and begins scooping a hole in the sand.

There are two burritos left. Miguel unwraps one and offers the other to Mr. Brewer.

"You go ahead," the man says. "I had a hell of a lunch." He carries a bottle of water to Papá and makes him drink before crouching to help dig.

Miguel thinks maybe he shouldn't eat either, that it's some custom the older men know and he doesn't, but his legs are shaking, and he feels like he'll pass out if he doesn't get at least a little food in his stomach. He eats only half of his burrito, barely anything, and wraps up the rest and puts it back in the bag.

The men are knee-deep in the grave when he finishes. Papá waves him off when he offers to help, but Mr. Brewer says he could use a break. Miguel replaces him in the hole and begins digging alongside his father.

Papá chuckles and says he can't believe it. He jokes about how Miguel has always hated having dirt on his hands, how even as a baby he'd run to Mamá when he got the littlest bit of mud on himself and cry and cry until she lifted him to the faucet and scrubbed his fingers clean. It's not funny to Miguel. *Why don't you look at me now, old man?* he thinks.

Papá refuses to take any breaks, but Miguel and Mr. Brewer switch off every few minutes. The ground beneath the sand is rock hard, so they pull the rubber tips off the crutches and use the crutches like jackhammers to bust up the soil. They work silently except for an occasional grunt or exhaled curse. Sweat runs down Miguel's face, and he licks his lips to taste it. Neither Papá nor Mr. Brewer admits to noticing when night falls, so Miguel doesn't comment either. The three of them continue digging in the dark.

Miguel is resting, lying on his back on a pile of freshly excavated dirt with his eyes closed, when Papá declares that they're finished. The hole is five feet deep. They chopped a step halfway up, which the old man and Mr. Brewer use now, Miguel pulling them the rest of the way out.

Papá sits for a while and drinks some water. He's covered from head to toe in dirt that's turned to mud wherever he sweats. He rinses his mouth and spits.

"I need you to bring the bones to me in the hole," he says to Miguel.

Miguel's heart stops.

"I can't," he says.

"Why not?"

"I can't touch them."

"It's your family."

Miguel doesn't respond; he's crying too hard. Deep, deep sobs, all of a sudden, out of nowhere. He's ashamed, but also angry. It's not normal, what the old man is asking. This isn't Mexico.

Mr. Brewer pats him on the back. "It's okay," he says, then walks over to the pile.

Mr. Brewer passes the remains to Papá, who stands in the grave and carefully lays them at his feet. Five minutes, and they've finished. Papá climbs out of the grave, and he and Mr. Brewer sit down to rest. Miguel feels like crying again. He and the old man will never be the same with each other, he knows. This day will forever stand between them.

Swallowing his grief, he walks over and begins shoveling dirt onto the bones with his hands.

"Wait, *mijo,* I'll help you," Papá says.

"I'm fine," Miguel replies, his voice too loud in the nighttime silence of the canyon. And then there's only the reassuring hymn of his breath and the grateful sigh of earth returning in darkness to where it belongs.

IT'S CLOSE TO midnight when they finish refilling the grave and stand over it with bowed heads. Brewer realizes he's forgotten all the prayers he ever knew except the childish ones, "Now I lay me down to sleep" and such, and decides he's fine with that.

Miguel is ready to walk out tonight, says he'll carry his dad if he has to. He's got school tomorrow, a track meet. Brewer argues the other side, pointing out how tricky the switchbacks will be for Armando on crutches, especially with no flashlight. Better to hunker down here until dawn, when it'll take half as long to make the climb and be a lot less dangerous. Miguel's face falls when Armando decides to wait. Brewer hates to see him disappointed. He's a good kid.

"A few more hours," he says to him.

The boy turns away, doesn't want to hear it.

The night is plenty warm, and there's food and enough water if they go easy on it. The three of them sit on the ground with their backs to the canyon wall, and Brewer smokes a cigarette. Lights twinkle in the distance. A ranch in Mexico, on the other side of the fence. The silence is so profound—everything that might make a noise having fled or been burned—that the distant roar of a jet passing high overhead makes them all look up.

Armando and Miguel stretch out on their backs, fingers laced behind their heads. Their breathing slows and deepens. Brewer won't be able to sleep without whiskey—that's the way it is these days—but he's content to sit and watch over the man and boy and wishes them peaceful dreams.

The stars do their dance for him, wheeling around a bright sliver of moon, and after making sure that all the constellations he knew as a boy are still there, he divides the sky into quadrants with an eye toward counting. Choosing a section, he begins: one star, two stars, three. He hopes

Cassius made it home, pictures the dog waiting for him when he returns to the trailer.

After an hour he dozes off and finds Charlie Wiggins fishing in a river he knows but can't name. His old friend draws his rod back, then snaps it forward, sending his lure into a dappled pool in the middle of the stream. Brewer is ecstatic watching him. *If this is forever,* he thinks, *I'm fine with it.* Suddenly, though, the light changes. The sun on the water burns brighter and brighter until Charlie is nothing but a silhouette against it, and Brewer is no longer able to distinguish his features. He reaches out to pull his friend into the shade with him, but no go. He wakes with a handful of sand and a too-familiar ache in his chest.

Armando has removed his jacket and covered Miguel with it and is sleeping with his arm wrapped protectively around the boy. Brewer is long past pondering how his life would have been different if certain things had happened or hadn't, but seeing father and son like this, he can't help but wonder about all that he missed that might have eased his way.

False dawn comes and goes, and the night seems somehow darker, colder, longer. Brewer is restless. He stands and walks, joints popping, to the edge of the flat, looks down canyon, then up toward the switchbacks they'll climb in the morning. A pale blue glow limns the east wall of the canyon, and the mound of sand marking the grave slowly becomes visible. The boy was seventeen, the girl sixteen. They died in each other's arms.

Alack, he was but one hour mine, Brewer thinks.

"You and your poems," Charlie Wiggins once said, lying beside him on a steamy summer evening in a room they shared.

Me and my poems, Brewer thinks now, and somewhere, way off in the unburned distance, a bird wakes and sings.

Acknowledgments

Thanks again to my agent, Henry Dunow; my editor, Asya Muchnick; and everybody at Little, Brown/Mulholland Books. Thanks to the publications in which some of these stories were originally published. And thanks to the John Simon Guggenheim Foundation and ECLA Aquitaine for financial support during the writing of this book.

About the Author

Richard Lange is the author of the story collection *Dead Boys,* which received the Rosenthal Family Foundation Award from the American Academy of Arts and Letters, and the novels *This Wicked World* and *Angel Baby,* which won the Hammett Prize from the International Association of Crime Writers. He is the recipient of a Guggenheim Fellowship, and his fiction has appeared in *The Best American Mystery Stories 2004* and *2011*. He lives in Los Angeles.